Volume One

Collected Stories

By Sam Holloway

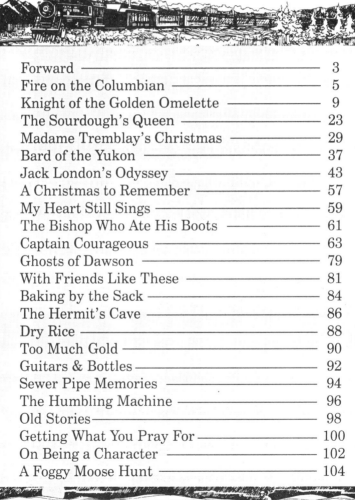

ISBN 0-9683719-0-6

2nd Printing, 2001

Published in Canada by:
THE YUKONER MAGAZINE
P.O. Box 15
Whitehorse, Yukon
Y1A 5X9
e-mail: info@yukoner.com
website: www.yukoner.com

For a current list of publications, please send for the latest issue of The Yukoner Magazine, at the address above. Price: $4.95, including postage, no GST. Visa accepted.

Tel./Fax (867) 660-5030

Forward

(written in 1987)

A few summers ago I came out of the Sixtymile Goldfields here in the Yukon as broke as I could be. I'd been working for some gold miners on a percentage basis. The company didn't turn up any gold in the sluice box and all our work was in vain. Ten percent of nothing is nothing.

So, in Dawson City one hot afternoon in August, I bumped into Tony Fritz, the oldest cabdriver in Canada.

"Zam!" he says, "I bane looking all ovah fa you! Two Englishmen, they vant to go goltpannink—undt Zam, they are rich!"

I met up with the Englishmen in the Downtown Hotel. Right out of Charles Dickens they were: old, baby-faced, pearshaped, excited.

"Well," I said, "I'll take you down along the Stewart River and we'll camp overnight. You're guaranteed some gold; depends on how hard you work. Have you got some gold pans? And how about a gun?"

"Gun!! Whatever for?"

"Bears. Maybe a mad moose. Or a pack of hungry wolves."

They looked at each other like delighted children.

"How much do you charge?"

"A fill-up of gas each way; a full-course meal everytime we go past the Klondike River Lodge; and one hundred dollars." We shook hands on the deal. Next morning, I picked them up at the hotel with their stuff. I was not impressed with their equipment. They had two little gold pans (the type sold in souvenir shops), two pairs of thin, white cotton gloves, two paper bags of bread and cookies, and a big thermos of tea. Turtleneck sweaters, funny little caps, and nonstop gabbing about their extensive experience in the tough spots of the world—yes, I knew I was in for a couple of rough days.

I threw everything into my old Fargo van and we headed south on the Klondike Highway. Rain drizzled down from a dark sky; a thick layer of mud greased the road; and we just kind of slithered along, taking our time . We stopped for steak and eggs at the Klondike River Lodge and then, some 80 miles out, I pulled off the highway onto a trail leading down to the Stewart River. Within 20 minutes we were far from the madding crowds. Now there was just the river, the trees, the rain drops, and us.

My favourite river, the Stewart. It just oils along through the big valley it dredged for itself, and there are good spirits in that valley.

I let the old fellows out, loaned them my gold pans, and showed them what to do. I could raise some 60 colours in every pan and they were coming up with about ten. They picked out the gold with tweezers and dropped these ever-so-tiny specks into a pickle jar they had brought along. The river being low, we could get right out to the sand bars. There, in some mud, fairly fresh grizzly tracks spraddled along for a ways. I called the Englishmen over for a look.

It dawned on them slowly that these tracks were for real! They fairly quivered with excitement and dread. They measured the tracks and the size of the griz's claws and took a lot of pictures. I got my old 30:06 out of the van and then we panned some more, cuddled up there on the riverbank like three conspirators.

Enough gold for now, they figured. I guess they each had about a dollar's worth. I built a big fire, heated up some water for tea and made some Spam sandwiches. It became quite dark—not real dark, just kind of dusky and gloomy like it does here in the Yukon in summer.

We stood around the fire and the old fellows weren't sleepy at all. I got my fold-up lawn chair out of the van; they sat on a log, and I commenced to tell them about the country:

How, right here on the Stewart River, men made their first decent gold finds in the Yukon, and how they went from here to discover the Klondike in 1896.

What Dawson was like in those days, how Swiftwater Bill could look over a piece of ground and tell if it was rich. How the whole country was full of crazy men, rich crazy men, and how the women came up from the south to take it all away from them.

And then I got telling them about bears and how to keep them away from your camp; and how not to get lost and about the Indians up here, how tough they were; and then I told them some of my own experiences of searching for gold all over the Yukon, and how the oldtimers lived...

"Why don't you write this all down?" they cried.

I took the old fellows back to town in the morning and they left, never to be seen in Dawson since. I thought about writing down some of the stuff I'd told them. I had to check up on a lot of things in the library and in the Archives at Whitehorse. Some of the stories have been told a thousand times but here they are again. And if you two Englishmen, I forget your names, should come across one of my stories, thank you for the idea.

Marsh Lake in winter.

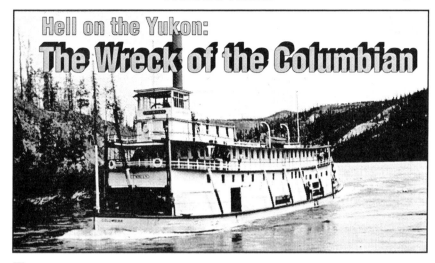

Hell on the Yukon:
The Wreck of the Columbian

Little Phil Murray, the deckboy, loved guns. Whenever the sternwheeler, the *Columbian*, stopped to take on cargo or firewood, little Phil would sneak away to shoot at squirrels, rabbits, anything that moved.

On September 25, 1906, as the steamer made its first voyage of the season between Whitehorse and Dawson, Phil was entranced by the flocks of geese and ducks that settled onto the river surface for the night. Against orders, he took out his repeating rifle and slipped in a cartridge. Standing beside him on the bow of the ship was another gun lover: Morgan, the fireman.

"Let me take a shot, Phil," he said.

Morgan grasped the rifle and took a step forward. His foot caught on a gangplank and he fell, right up against a stack of blasting powder. The gun went off.

Altogether, three tons of powder stacked in iron kegs covered the front cargo deck of the Columbian.

The sternwheeler, which belonged to White Pass, had no passengers this trip because of the dangerous cargo—except for one: a stowaway named Wynstanley. He had sneaked aboard with 25 cattle, pretending to be their caretaker. He was to be thrown off at Tantalus.

Up in the wheelhouse, the skipper, J. O. Williams, contemplated the next stop at the Tantalus Coal Mine (near Carmacks) where he would get rid of the explosives. In appearance, Captain Williams was very ordinary: slim build, medium height, with a slightly oversized moustache. The captain of a ship, whether it floats on a river or on the rolling ocean, plays the part of a minor god. Nothing happens without his orders or plan. Along with this authority goes the ultimate responsibility. He is to blame for the mistakes of his crew. He is in charge of all disasters.

Without warning, a great blast of heat and flame blew in the windows of the wheelhouse and knocked Captain Williams backward onto the floor. Quickly, though singed and covered with broken glass, he sprang to his feet and tried to steer the boat ashore. Nothing worked—the steering gear, the voice tube to the engine room, the engine signal—all were dead in his hands.

And so the Columbian, 147 feet long, 33 feet wide, capable of carrying 175 passengers plus freight, sped downstream in the evening twilight with every deck ablaze. All around her debris from the shattered power kegs splashed onto the surface of the river.

Captain Williams kicked the wheelhouse door open. Out on the "Texas" deck he met the pilot who had climbed up from the galley (dining room) to be at his fire station. Down below, members of the crew of 25 fought the blaze at their fire stations while others tried to free the lifeboats. The lifeboats were already afire and the canvas fire hoses burned and burst in the hands of the crew. The ship's engines hadn't missed a beat and kept her steaming full speed ahead. The engineer, dashing about midst the smoke and fire, awaited orders from his captain.

The captain knew if he couldn't land his ship within a few minutes, all aboard would roast or else drown in the freezing waters of the Yukon. He grabbed a rope and slid down it to land amongst flames and smoke on the lower deck. Somewhere he heard the muffled screams of a man in terrible agony. He ran to the engine room and shouted for Mavis the engineer to stop the engines.

"Be ready to give her half-speed when I yell," said the captain.

Just downstream was a bend in the river. As they came into it Captain Williams yelled and in a moment the bow of the boat crashed into the shore. The men still alive

Captain J.O. Williams

on the bow jumped ashore before the current swung the boat around.

"Full speed astern! Keep her there even if you tear the buckets out of her!" screamed the captain to the engineer.

The great paddlewheel clawed its way up onto the bank. The skipper and two deckhands grabbed a wire cable and jumped overboard with it. They floundered to shore in the chest-high water and fastened the cable to a tree. Then the captain rushed back to the ship to give his last order to the engineer.

"Shut her down and get yourself to hell out of there!"

Up on shore Captain Williams counted the survivors. Morgan, the man who had fired the fateful shot, and Welch, the mate, were the only ones who hadn't made it out. The captain started for the boat to look for them but some of his men held onto him. As they tussled on the bank, the texas deck caved in and crashed through the main deck, making further search useless.

All of the six crewmen who had been standing closest to the blasting powder were mortally damaged by the flames. Rather than a terrific explosion, the powder had created a firestorm which sent a blinding sheet of flame racing the full length of the ship. Luckily, most of the men stood out of the direct path of the flame.

Little Phil and Woods the deckhand had all of their clothing blown off them by the blast and their bodies horribly blackened. Coal trimmer Smith had stumbled into the engine room, on fire from head to foot. The engineer coated his body with cylinder oil and helped carry Smith ashore. Cowper the purser and Wynstanley the stowaway were the least injured of the group. Of the two men unaccounted for, no trace of Morgan was ever found, but Welch's body turned up the river two months later.

The captain looked around at his little group, at the men lying among the willows moaning from their terrible wounds. They had no blankets, food, medicine, boats, lanterns, nothing at all. He sent two men upstream to Little Salmon, nine miles away. They returned in the morning with a boat and a few supplies. The big job was to get to the telegraph station, 30 miles away at Tantalus.

For this task he picked Second Mate Smith and two others. They followed the riverbank on foot for a couple of miles and realized they were travelling too slow. Using belts and suspenders, they rigged a tiny raft upon which Smith floated downstream with most of the raft submerged and with his legs dangling in the icy water. He nearly made it to Tantalus but was overtaken by Captain Williams and Engineer

Mavis riding in a canoe they had borrowed from a woodcutter.

They hauled Smith aboard and pushed on for Tantalus, arriving there shortly after midnight. They woke up the telegraph operator who immediately tapped out the terrible news over the line. They waited anxiously for a response—but none came.

All the operators were asleep, even at the metropolis of Dawson City. The first to receive the story and the call for help was the operator at Whitehorse but it was nine o'clock in the morning.

Having done all he could, Captain Williams decided to return to the Columbian with supplies and medicine in the middle of the night. The people from the coal mine made up three packs of 50 pounds each for the captain and his crew of two. The canoe would not carry them and their load upstream so they went overland through brush and muskeg and timber, there being no trail at all.

First, though, they tried to borrow a horse from the local Mounted Police constable. The Mountie said, "No way, not without orders from headquarters." Disgusted, they left him wishing they had just taken a horse (the Mountie had several) and asked later. The constable slammed the door and went back to his sleep.

Two miners accompanied them for five miles and then the sailors were on their own. They fought their way through thick brush, across small creeks, through dense bush full of deadfalls, staying close to the river so as not to lose their way in the semi-darkness. Ten hours after setting out they arrived at the wreck.

Coal trimmer Smith and Woods, the deckhand, had died during the night. Little Phil Murray, still a favourite among the crew in spite of being responsible for their plight, hung on though suffering terrible. His father, pilot on the Bonanza King, was on his way to see Phil, they told him, and he made no complaint except to ask, "Is my daddy here yet?"

But it was the sternwheeler Victorian that arrived first. Bound upstream with a barge, she received the news only that afternoon and had raced full speed to pick up the survivors. It was now 7.00 p. m., the day after the explosion. From Whitehorse another boat, the Dawson, was dispatched carrying a doctor and nurses.

When little Phil heard the chugging of the Victorian he brightened, expecting to see his father. After being carried aboard and realizing it was not his father's boat, he seemed to lose interest in living. His breaths came slower and slower and he died a few minutes later.

Meanwhile the Dawson was racing downstream under every pound of steam her boiler could carry. Her captain had not received the news until he and his ship arrived at Whitehorse at one o'clock that afternoon, September 26. With pilot George Raabe at the wheel, the Dawson ran the Thirty-mile River (the stretch of the Yukon between Lake Laberge and the Teslin River) at full speed and without a single "slow bell." No other steamboat made the run as fast as the Dawson did that day. At one o'clock the following morning, September 27, the Dawson met the Victorian and took the crew of the Columbian on board.

Purser Cowper died soon after arriving at Whitehorse. Of the seven men who had been standing close to the powder kegs, only Wynstanley, the stowaway, survived.

In the Whitehorse Cemetery, a monument was erected bearing the names of the men who died.

It was said that great packs of wolves came along to fight over and devour the dead cattle from the Columbian, and that folks salvaged supplies for months afterward.

The Columbian wreckage. [Yukon Archives photo, Muirhead collection]

The Salty Saga of Swift Water Bill

W. C. Gates lived out the fantasies of a repressed society, during an age when piano legs were draped with cloth to cover their "nakedness." In his pursuit of gold, fame and women, he had more successes—and failures— than any man in the history of the North.

The first half of Bill's life was easy to research because the press followed his every move. In one instance they sifted the ashes in his hotel fireplace for evidence of his sinning.

His disappearance from North America left most historians with little information to cover his later years. Now, thanks to an Alaskan prospector, the rest of Bill's adventures have come to light. So here is the story, too outlandish for fiction or film—but true—of "Swiftwater" Bill Gates...

Alaska, 1896

Originally from Redwing, Minnesota, Bill first came into the Yukon sometime in 1895. He had played around with prospecting in the central States and had worked in a copper mine in Idaho. It was there that he heard about the gold discoveries in Alaska.

In 1896, Bill was washing dishes and making beds at a crudely-built log hostel in Circle City, Alaska. One night after supper, as he was cleaning up the dining hall, he overheard two men talking about the big gold strike in the Klondike.

Misty dawn found Bill poling a flat-bottomed boat upstream toward Dawson, 275 miles away. It was no easy feat. The Yukon River runs swift and the poler, using all his limbs and back to move against the current, must stay near shore in the shallow water. Hordes of flies and mosquitoes can attack him unmercifully.

Miles Canyon

Bill knew how to handle boats, however. He often bragged of this ability and his pals dubbed him "Swiftwater Bill."

His detractors—of which he was to have many—told a different story. They said that on his initial entry to the Yukon, Swiftwater jumped out of the boat and walked around the notorious Miles Canyon and Whitehorse Rapids. After his companions put the boat through the turbulent waters, Swiftwater rejoined the expedition. And that, according to them, was how he came by his nickname.

His later adventures in the Yukon and on the upper rivers of the Amazon jungle lend more credence to the first story than the latter. Whatever the case, he did stand out from his peers by the very contrast he presented to them.

The men along the Yukon in those days were a hardy lot—perhaps the toughest, fiercest at work

or play, most macho white men on the continent—while Bill was a short, small-limbed waif of a man. His slight paunch and indolent manner bespoke his aversion to hard work and danger. He sported an enormous black moustache and, in the manner of many small men, he spoke with a strident timbre when bragging of his accomplishments and bravery. No one took him very seriously.

Swiftwater strikes it rich...

All the claims along Bonanza and Eldorado Creeks had been staked by the time Bill arrived from Alaska but he and six others obtained a lay on Claim #13, Eldorado. They worked together to put a shaft down to bedrock and whooped for joy at what they found—coarse gold in a paystreak that seemed of endless width and length. At Bill's urging they covered up the incredible find and went to the owner of the claim with a joint offer of $40,000. They were willing to take a chance if he would sell this claim with the unlucky number.

The owner fell for it and the boys soon brought him enough gold to pay off their debt. Before long Bill's (and the others') pockets and packsacks bulged with gold.

Into town he went, $20,000 richer, and hired newcomers to work his ground on a percentage basis. He then bought the best clothes he could find in Dawson and sported the only starched collar in town. Mining camp followers were descending on the Klondike from all over Alaska and these included quite a few hurdy-gurdy girls. In his princely manner, Swiftwater brought coveys of these females out to his claim to help themselves to some of his gold. He bought all the love and laughter that was available in the embryo town—even if they were laughing at him.

He loved to gamble. Never a heavy drinker, he gambled on any game he came across. He lost more often than he won. When he strutted into a saloon he yelled loud enough to be heard above the roar of the crowd:

"De sky's de limit boys! And if de roof's in your way, why just tear it off!"

When professional theatre entertainment arrived in Dawson, one company staged a satire entitled, *"The Adventures of Stillwater Willie."* Bill revelled in the attention it brought him and attended every performance. No one could say for sure whether the crowd laughed at him or at the show, but he minded not at all. Swiftwater Bill provided a spectacle in a town full of eccentrics. In his swan-tailed coat and diamond cravat, with his devilish black eyes and flowing moustache, he outshone all others in those heady days of easy fortune in the Yukon.

He met a man operating a saloon about a mile from town. The man's name was Jack Smith. Jack had come down from Fortymile with his variety troupe. He had staked a rich claim, sold it for $150,000, and was moving on to bigger and better endeavours.

He and Bill decided to build what was to become the most glittering pleasure palace ever to be seen in the North: the Monte Carlo Dance Hall & Saloon. While Jack looked after construction he entrusted Bill with the chore of going "outside" for a load of furniture, liquor and dancing girls.

In the days to come Jack Smith was to bitterly regret this decision.

Jack Smith (centre) and Swiftwater (second from right) posing in front of the Bonanza Saloon. This establishment was said to have taken in up to one hundred ounces of gold per night during its heyday in the early days in the Klondike. [Photo reproduced from The Klondike News, April 1, 1898]

Swiftwater and the eggs...

Meanwhile, Swiftwater began a stormy courtship of a buxom, platinum-blonde dance hall girl called Gussie Lamore. Gussie was the reigning queen of the muddy town and billed herself as *"The Little Klondike Nugget."* Bill offered Gussie her weight in gold if she would marry him. She stalled him by saying she was "not quite ready yet." (Unknown to Bill, she was married and had a three-year-old child.) One night he saw her dancing merrily with a big French Canadian. The ensuing argument touched off a legend that would earn Bill a new title: "The Knight of the Golden Omelette."

The story flashed up and down the creeks, from cabin to cabin, from camp to camp, from saloon to saloon until the whole Yukon knew the story, one version of it or another.

Gussie Lamore loved eggs. She could never get enough of them in Dawson, simply because there weren't any. Just about the time of her argument with Bill, a shipment of eggs came into town by dogteam. Swiftwater bought them all, some 2,200 eggs at a dollar each. And that's what started the stories.

Arthur Walden, the well-known dogpuncher, said in his memoirs that Bill had the eggs fried in a restaurant and then threw them out, one at a time, to the dogs in the street.

Stroller White, the famous news columnist, said Bill kept the eggs under his bed at the hotel till they all turned rotten.

Others said Bill invited every dance hall girl in town for a feast of eggs, all except Gussie.

The Klondike Nugget dubbed Swiftwater *"The Knight of the Golden Omelette."*

Bill never talked about it at all. Some years later Gussie told the real story to a news reporter in Seattle:

"I met Swiftwater," she said, "in Dawson of '97. He certainly had the coin then. He lavished money on me but I got dead sick of him. He had no sense so I got to skating around with another guy. There was an egg famine come on in Dawson. I'd shaken Bill.

"I went down to the store to buy some eggs...Lordy how I wanted some eggs for breakfast. Well, Bill was in the store when I goes in. He sees I wanted the eggs and while I'm talking to the clerk, see, he buys up the whole consignment of 900 eggs at $1 apiece. Then he says to me, 'Now my dear, if you want eggs for breakfast, come home where you belong.'

"Well, I was just dying for them eggs, and I came to my milk like a lady. I goes home with Bill."

In the fall of 1897, Bill and a new friend of his, Joseph Whiteside Boyle (who would one day become a true Klondike King), Indian Charlie, and few others left Dawson for the "outside." Swift was to come back from the south with all the necessities for the Monte Carlo: booze, furnishings and, most important, women.

It was a hell of a trip for them. They poled a boat upstream until the river froze and had to wait a month at Stewart Island until the ice was solid enough to walk on. At last they were able to resume the journey but somewhere on the river Swiftwater broke through the ice and big Joe Boyle fished him out.

Leaving the river, they hiked over the Dalton Trail to Haines Mission. The hundred-mile journey normally took about four days but in the extreme cold and snowstorms they struggled for 25 days before reaching the coast. Some of the party wanted to just "lay down and die." Swiftwater and Joe Boyle urged them on. At last they boarded a ship and arrived in Seattle on November 29th, two full months after leaving the Klondike.

Gussie Lamore, wise to the ways of the North, went over the ice that winter as a passenger in a dog sled. She met up with Bill in San Francisco.

Klondike fever was just beginning in the west coast cities and Swiftwater was living proof of the riches to be had. He passed out large nuggets to the bellhops at his hotel to tell all comers that the man in the fur hat was *"Swiftwater Bill Gates, King of the Klondike."*

Gussie took her well-dressed beau to meet her folks. Years later she told the story to the Seattle Washingtonian:

"In 'Frisco I introduced Bill to my family. Well, say, would you believe it, my sister Grace she cops him

Swiftwater (right) and Joe Boyle, setting out from the Klondike in 1897.

out—steals him from me cold and marries him.

"Well, say, she lives with him a couple of weeks and quits him. She couldn't stand him at all. She leaves their rooms at the Baldwin and takes a flat. Bill, he goes to her room while she's away, wraps her silverware and other valuables in a sheet and carries them downtown on his back.

No woman could live with Bill...

Finally Grace she gets a divorce and her maiden name back and then, he steps in and joins up with my sister Nell.

"Nell only lived with him for a week. Then Bill tried to cop out this fourth sister of mine after Nellie shook him but he couldn't touch her with a ten-foot pole. That's where she's wiser than the rest of us.

"No woman could live with Bill. He's one of those camp guys that never had any money in his life till he got a great big bunch of it all at once. He doesn't know nuthin' except to tell everybody he's lousy with the yellow stuff. He'd throw dollars into the crowds just to see 'em scramble and let 'em know he had it to trown (sic) at the birds. He'd tip bellboys with $5 gold pieces and buy wine at show prices by the barrel."

"Hasn't a particle of intellect; couldn't carry on a conversation to save his soul. He's no company for a woman and still he's jealous if a woman only looks at another man."

"Say, did you ever see his get-up? Well, you ought to. He wears a plug hat of the vintage of '75; then he wears a Prince Albert coat and a negligee shirt that cost him a dollar and a quarter. He tops the whole thing out with dancing pumps. Why say, he's a regular mark."

From then until the day he left North America, newspapers tracked Bill's every move. They delightedly reported on his affairs with the Lamore sisters. What they could not find out directly they made up from the slightest rumours. Even up north in Dawson the Klondike Nugget said Bill had "bought Grace Lamore a huge white mansion" and after the breakup he "made off with $7,000 worth of wedding gifts." With his love of exaggeration and the newspapers' wild reporting, the legend of Swiftwater Bill, the Klondike Prince, grew and grew. His name was a household word all over the U. S. and Canada.

Jack Smith in Dawson cringed every time he read a new story about his "partner."

Bill's money was fast running out. Not one item had yet been purchased for the Monte Carlo. The Lamore sisters had taken him for about $100,000 and his every action as a Klondike King cost plenty. He holed up at the Palace Hotel in San Francisco, keeping a low profile. About this time a rich doctor came to see the "famous mining magnate" at his suite of rooms.

Swiftwater regaled Doctor Wolf with tales of the Klondike and painted a glowing portrait of the opportunities there for someone with money to invest. Quickly they formed a partnership. Together they would create a vast trading and transportation network stretching from Skagway to Circle City. In the meantime could the doctor advance Bill some funds? At one hundred percent interest?

With $20,000 of Doctor Wolf's

money in his pocket, Swiftwater took off to Seattle. In that fair city, which was the main jumping off point for the Klondike stampeders, he set about gathering supply contracts for the new business. At the same time he rounded up a group of women to work in the Monte Carlo and bought furnishings and supplies—mostly on credit.

The winter of 1898 was half over. The entire world knew about the gold in the Klondike and some 100,000 people made plans to go there. The supplies and services they bought gave a tremendous boost to the cities along the west coast. In the midst of all this bustle Swiftwater showed them that a man really could come out of the Klondike with a fortune—and then just go back for more.

Around and around Seattle he paraded, surrounded by a group of attractive women. Very few knew that these laughing members of his "harem" were on the payroll of the Monte Carlo. In his Klondike costume—fur hat, parka, mukluks—he caused a sensation wherever he went.

After one party at the ritzy Rainier-Grand Hotel the management presented him with a bill for damages amounting to $1,500.

He bought champagne by the case and invited reporters to watch him bathe in it. When one reporter asked for an exclusive interview, Bill told him it would cost him $1,000 a minute.

Doctor Wolf, seeing all the stories in the papers, sent word for Bill to hurry up with the arrangements so they could be on their way to the Klondike.

Bill planned to leave soon any-

how. He was again running low on funds. He and his "staff" boarded a ship for Skagway. They partied all the way under the disapproving glares of Doctor Wolf. They had to wait for a month in Skagway for the Yukon River system to thaw and had another wonderful time as they waited. Doctor Wolf hired a dogteam to take him over the ice to Dawson. Soon after he arrived there he heard some very disturbing rumours about his partner.

Jack Smith flew into a rage every time someone mentioned Swiftwater Bill. Eugene Allen, editor of the *Klondike Nugget* newspaper, had this to say:

"Swiftwater has never been known to pay back any money after it was thrown away. If he made another lucky strike somewhere, he might toss some your way, but that's about your only chance."

Return to the Klondike...

One day the word flew around the City of Gold: Swiftwater Bill Gates and his party were just upstream, round the big bend in the Yukon River. They would be arriving at any moment. Soon a large crowd milled about on the waterfront.

They were well rewarded for their patience. In the prow of a Peterborough canoe stood Swiftwater, posing grandly, all decked out in his Prince Albert coat and silk top hat. Beside him a dance hall girl perched beautifully on a whiskey keg. Behind the canoe came two barges piled high with crates. On these crates sat many more smiling, painted women wearing low-cut evening gowns. The men on shore cheered wildly, the girls waved back at them, and when the convoy nudged into the dock, all the men pitched in to help the girls ashore.

In the meantime, Jack Smith and Doctor Wolf were elbowing their way through the crowd. They grabbed Bill from both sides.

"Swiftwater!" roared the doctor, his face red as a beet. *"You've got exactly three hours to pay back the twenty thousand! Never mind the interest! Just get my goddam money!"*

Somehow Bill borrowed enough money to pay the doctor, sans interest, and arranged to turn his share of the Monte Carlo and some earnings from his claim over to Jack Smith. He was clear of his creditors and then sold his interest in the Eldorado claim. He still had a claim on Sulphur Creek and was ready for some new action.

He staked out a three-mile mining concession on Quartz Creek. Joe Boyle did the same on other creeks and somehow they obtained title from the Canadian government in Ottawa. Partners now, the two of them sailed to London, England, to raise capital for the first large-scale mining operation in the Yukon.

Swiftwater and Boyle formed an odd couple. Bill was tiny and ostentatious while Joe Boyle was a big, quiet man who needed no fancy attire or braggadocio to prove his manhood. While Boyle attended to business, Swiftwater caused a sensation in the courts of Europe.

Swiftwater dazzles Europe..

Dubbed the *Klondike Prince* in the press, Bill told reporters he would bet $7,000 with any comer on one turn of a card. He visited Paris where beautiful women swooned over this flashy "millionaire" from the wild frontier. Finally Joe Boyle sent Bill and a British mining expert to San Francisco where they were to arrange the purchase and shipment of mining equipment to the Klondike. Attended to by barbers and shoeshine boys, Swiftwater again became the most celebrated man in the city.

About this time a woman planning to ship a hotel piecemeal to Dawson City visited Bill at his hotel. She wanted some expert advice on conditions in the North. She was Iola Beebe, an attractive, matronly widow with two beautiful daughters.

For the rest of her life she would lament the day she introduced herself and her daughters to Swiftwater Bill Gates.

While Mrs. Beebe explained her plans, Bill gazed lecherously at 19-year-old Blanch. His business associate, the British mining engineer, lent such an air of respectability to this little group that Mrs. Beebe had no suspicion of the undercurrents of lust flowing beneath all the talk. She received the first of many great awakenings when she found the following note on her mantel:

"Dear Mama. We have gone to Alaska with Swiftwater and Mr. Hathaway. Do not worry, we will look out for your hotel when we get there. Bera."

Bera was 15 years old at the time. The hysterical Mrs. Beebe stormed onto the steamer Humboldt, which was just about to depart for Alaska, and found her girls in a cabin. Swiftwater hid under a lifeboat but the ship's officers located him. The police were summoned and the captain of the ship chafed at the delay while Bill gently persuaded Mrs. Beebe of the honour of his character.

She agreed to let the ship sail—minus her daughters. They all met up again in Skagway a few weeks later. Mrs. Beebe watched over her girls night and day but to no avail. She found another note in her room:

"Dear mama. I have gone to Dawson with Swiftwater. He loves me and I love him. Bera."

The chase was on.

Mrs. Beebe arrived in Dawson to be met on the dock by Bill and Bera, who were now husband and wife. Marriage sanctified the whole relationship—so much so that Bill soon had $35,000 of his mother-in-law's money invested in his mining operation. They all moved out to Sulphur Creek for the winter and Bera gave birth to a son.

Alas, things were not working out for Bill. His gambling and mining debts piled up. He flirted with Gussie Lamore who sang to him from her spot on the stage but he couldn't take her up on the offer without money, lots of money. (She would sing an old song, *"He Certainly Was Good to Me"* to the delight of the crowd. Of course Bill sent up champagne to the cast, as any good sport should.)

He bought a small boat, packed Bera into it, and they set out for the ruby sands of Nome, leaving behind a destitute mother-in-law, the baby, and $100,000 worth of bills. Too broke to follow her slippery son-in-law, Mrs. Beebe existed on charity until she received a letter from Swiftwater. He had recouped his fortunes on Dexter Creek just out of Nome and she must join them there as soon as possible.

Off she went, down the Yukon

On Quartz Creek. Left to right, Black servant, Iola Beebe, Bera Beebe, Swiftwater, a doctor hired to deliver Bera's baby. Notice how well-dressed they are in the roughness of their cabin and surroundings. Bill is wearing a suit and necktie, but on his feet he has high, wading type rubber boots. (Yukon Archives photo)

River by sternwheeler. The trip was long—long enough for her to hear that Bill was gambling heavily—and losing. When she finally stepped ashore at Nome, Swiftwater was gone. In fact, a Seattle newspaper had already arrived and there was Bill in the headlines:

SWIFTWATER BILL RUNS AWAY WITH ANOTHER WOMAN!

Indeed, he had covered a lot of ground while Mrs. Beebe had been on her 1500-mile trip down the Yukon River. He had left Nome with Bera. It was now fall, 1900, and they went to Washington where he happened to meet up with his sister's step-daughter, Kitty Brandon, at an Elk's carnival in Tacoma. In love again, he abandoned the pregnant Bera and eloped with Kitty, who was 16 years old at the time. The couple honeymooned at a posh hotel in Seattle.

In the meantime Mrs. Beebe had arrived on the coast. Now three furious women were searching everywhere for Swiftwater: Bera, Bill's sister, and of course Iola Beebe. It was his sister who caught up to him first.

Bill looked down from his hotel room window and spotted his sister rushing up the steps to the lobby. Quickly he and Kitty scrambled down a fire escape and went back to Tacoma. Leaving her behind, Bill rode a train to Butte, Montana.

Who should be there but Gussie Lamore, just home from Dawson. She and her sister Belle were singing at a local nightclub. Bill signed over a part interest in a Nome gold claim to Gussie and she let it be known that she and her old love might marry. Suddenly Belle Lamore and Swift went missing from Butte, Montana. Soon Gussie received a wire from her sister: Belle and Swift had married and chartered a Pullman car for New York City.

This marriage (he now had three official wives) cooled off very fast and Bill drifted back to Alaska, this time to the Valdez area where he took up prospecting again.

For once he had poor luck and using an assumed name (Williams), he returned south and holed up in a room at the Victoria Hotel in Seattle.

Bill recoups his fortunes...

His reverie of self pity was shattered by a loud pounding on the door. He opened it just a crack and staggered backward. Mrs. Iola Beebe shoved the door open and flounced into the room.

Partially naked, Bill leaped onto the bed and pulled the covers up over his face. In the meantime his mother-in-law screeched out all the bitterness that boiled inside her. He beseeched her to leave him alone. He was finished, he said, all washed up and ready to die.

When at length she took a good look at the scruffy, sorrowful-looking waif on the bed, her maternal instincts awakened (or was it something else?) in spite of her anger. Bill quickly noticed the softening of her resolve. Soon he had her listening raptly to his tale of woe: how sorry he was for his mistakes and how he had only one chance to make amends—that was to head north again to the newly discovered Tanana River goldfields in Alaska.

Mrs. Beebe went out and pawned her jewellery to grubstake the new adventure. Afterwards she was amazed at how quickly Swiftwater became his former self.

From Dawson City he hiked over the trail to the headwaters of the Tanana River. He was seen tramping into Fairbanks wearing one rubber boot, one rubber overshoe, and his old yellow mackinaw. There, among many old cronies from the early rush into the Klondike, Bill obtained a partial interest in a couple of claims on Cleary Creek. They turned out to be incredibly rich.

A small settlement grew up around his claims. They named it Gates City, in honour of Bill who, besides his womanizing and gambling, was famous for being able to spot a likely piece of ground. Word of his new fortune got around. Soon, two very determined women waited in Fairbanks for him to come out of the bush—-Iola Beebe and Bill's sister (the stepmother of Kitty Brandon).

Packing a suitcase full of gold, Swiftwater boarded a sternwheeler for the coast. Mrs. Beebe, now well-tuned to his devious ways, booked passage on the same boat. She kept her eyes on him for the entire journey. At St. Michael, Alaska, they changed to a ship and again she never let Bill out of her sight.

A lecherous monster...

When they reached Seattle, Swiftwater jumped onto a barge and then to shore before the ship was fully docked. Mrs. Beebe set police and private detectives on his trail. They scooted him out of a Seattle bar and into jail went Swiftwater; the charge, bigamy.

He had hidden his gold and Mrs. Beebe couldn't touch his mining claims. Through prison bars he persuaded her to bail him out. He would retrieve his gold, pay her some money, and straighten out his affairs. Part of the deal was that Bera must grant him a divorce so he could shake the bigamy charge.

Mrs. Beebe arranged everything and Bill was let out of prison. He eloped again—with Kitty Brandon. So far Mrs. Beebe hadn't received a penny from her slippery son-in-law.

Incredulous reporters sought her out for the story. The ensuing newspaper coverage must surely have encouraged other mothers-in-law to look more kindly on the men their own daughters had married.

Swiftwater divorced Kitty and went back to his claim in Alaska. Mrs. Beebe, upon learning that he

I found this picture among a collection of photos at Jim Robb's house one evening. Immediately I recognized old Swift. Who but he would wear such an outfit on a mining claim? Since the photo was published in the *Yukon Reader*, it has been used in various publications and in a film. S.H.

had taken another $200,000 worth of gold from the ground, decided to make another attempt to gain redress from Bill—the man who had ruined her life. She caught up to him on a side street in Fairbanks.

She grabbed him and shook him like a mother would an errant child. He pulled $50 from his pocket and as she reached for the money he slipped away from her and ran off down the street.

That was the last time Mrs. Beebe ever saw Swiftwater Bill Gates. Somehow he clambered aboard a departing boat and returned to the south where he declared bankruptcy.

He had already signed his claim over to a friend in Fairbanks. Unable to touch his resources, his mother-in-law garnered some measure of revenge by publishing a book on Swiftwater. The book described Bill as nothing more than a *"cowardly, dastardly scalawag"* and a *"lecherous monster."*

Swiftwater Bill joined a silver rush to Peru after that. He was only seen in the U. S. a few more times, and never again after 1908. His name disappeared from the press.

Epilogue

In spite of his prowess in the mining business and his abilities in the northern wilderness, folks always thought of Bill as being something less than a real man.

They laughed at his clothes, his many marriages, his gambling, his escapades. Yet, in many respects he was a gentleman. He took the insults and exaggerations with good humour and went on looking for gold or for another wife. When he

disappeared from North America around 1910, the newspapers—who had hounded him so mercilessly—forgot about him. But the stories about Swiftwater lived on, repeated in almost every book dealing with the Klondike Gold Rush. Even today books are going into print that rehash the old stories about Swiftwater, most of them only partly true.

In 1985, I wrote to various historians and to newspapers and libraries, to everyone I could think of. Whatever became of Swiftwater Bill? No one seemed to know. The only clue was a picture and short death notice that appeared in the August, 1950, edition of the *Alaska Weekly*. Further checking proved the picture to be of Bill McKay, an Alaskan state senator who came to the Klondike in 1898.

In 1986, I received a letter from Fairbanks, Alaska. It was from Paolo Greer, an Alaskan prospector and adventurer who had given lectures and slide presentations on his expeditions to Peru. Paolo had called at the office of the *Fairbanks Daily News-Miner* just as my letter requesting information on Swiftwater had arrived at the editor's desk.

Would I like to know, asked Paolo in his letter, about the final years of Swiftwater Bill? He had just returned from Peru and had some information. I answered right away. Soon I received a package containing pictures, magazine articles (from Peru), old letters, etc. from which I pieced together the story.

Swiftwater was murdered on February 21, 1937, twenty-eight years after he was last seen in Alaska. The shooting took place in a tiny hut on the Tunquimayo Tributary of the Nusiniscato River in the Quispicanchi District of Southeastern Peru.

A young man named Eduardo Gonzales called Swiftwater up to the sleeping loft of the hut. When Bill's head appeared at the top of the ladder, Gonzales blasted him with a heavy-gauge shotgun.

Eduardo was one of two brothers working for Bill. They killed him for his gold—which they didn't find hidden under the bed—and his tools. The brothers disappeared after the killing and were never seen in the district again.

At the time of his death Swift was 68 years old. He was still prospecting and mining and had big plans for the future. The State Department found it convenient to call the death accidental rather than investigate the murder of another "gringo."

The cabin where Bill was shot no longer stands. His grave site close by was long ago dug up and run through a sluice box, a very fitting tribute to a man whose life always centered around gold.

The three little jars of gold under Swiftwater's bed had been saved by him for a project dear to his heart: he was going to take his daughter, Lydia, to the U.S.A. where they would find her a gringo husband. Swift had met Lydia's mother, Victoria, in 1917 and took her to the jungle with him where Lydia was born. Bill might have married Victoria, who was 16 when he met her, but her parents disapproved of him and would not consent.

Swiftwater, age 63 (right), and Clarence Woods panning for gold in Peru.

Lydia last heard from her father in late January, 1937. He wrote her a letter telling her not to buy clothes or anything; they would obtain everything in the U.S, It was the last anyone heard from the one-time greatest high roller of the north.

Swift had other women during his 27 years in the jungle. The press couldn't follow him around like they did in North America so there aren't many details in print. He did have a son by a woman, Marina, in Aporoma, Peru. In general folks said that Bill was a generous man who had no enemies and that "la ruina de Gates era el juego" (Gates' ruin was gambling).

It can be safely conjectured that from 1910 till his death in 1937, Bill had found his niche in life—mining, guiding the occasional exploration party, chasing young women, gambling, and scouring the Amazon jungle for another big strike—which he never found. In North America he went to great lengths to prove to the world that he was a man in spite of his faults. Down here in the jungle that sort of stuff didn't matter.

He was influential in bringing the first big gold dredges into the country and taught his prospecting skills to anyone interested.

The upper Amazon River country, where Bill spent the best years of his life, is a dark forest intersected by countless rivers and smaller streams. Sharp vines, lightning quick vipers, anaconda snakes a foot thick, armor-plated scorpions—with legs and antennae a foot long with lobster-like claws—ants almost two inches long, tropical warble flies, legions of biting insects, rabid vampire bats, voracious piranha fish—these are just a few of the hazards he faced on his travels through the jungle. Yet he did so as easily as any native.

The story of Swiftwater is an age-old tale: a man finds gold, squanders the riches from it, then searches for more. Soon the search itself becomes the all-important motif in his life. All else—sex, material possessions, fame, whatever, are only temporary diversions from the search. Robert Service, Bard of the Yukon, explained it better than anyone:

*"...it isn't the gold that I'm wanting,
So much as just finding the gold."*

*****

Notes:

The photo of Swiftwater panning for gold came from Clarence Woods, grandson of another Clarence Woods who is also in the photo. Clarence Woods was Swiftwater's one-time partner in Peru. Swiftwater, who was quite portly in his later years, looks very gaunt and thin in this picture, likely because of swamp fever.

There was another photo of Bill in an issue of the National Geographic, published in the early 1930s.

Again, thank you Paolo Greer for the information in this epilogue.

Swift Water Bill

A copy of Bill's signature. Note that he separated the words "Swift" and "Water" although writers have always joined the two words. S.H.

Klondike Kate

Klondike Kate was the Yukon's first sex symbol. I started researching her story in the Yukon Archives and amongst old books and newspapers; I wanted to know why they called her the Queen of the Klondike, Flower of the North, the Darling of Dawson, and all the other names she had.

It wasn't long before I realized the truth: Kate was a self-promoter—a very good self promoter. Many writers fell for her line of gab and so a legend was born.

A lot of people try to make themselves into characters. It's as if they try to make up on the outside for the blankness inside. But Klondike Kate was different. Underneath all the hype and phony romance there was a real character and a story after all.

Kate Rockwell

She was born Kathleen Rockwell in a little town called Junction City, Kansas, on October 4th, 1876. She got into theatre work as a teenager which, in the opinion of decent folk then, was just slightly better than being a whore. In the spring of 1900—by now she was 24—she had a chance to go into the Klondike with the Savoy Theatrical Company of Vancouver. The Gold Rush had been over for almost two years, but there were still some big spenders left in Dawson City.

By 1900 Dawson had grown from a haphazard gathering of

shacks and log buildings into a modern city. They called it the Paris of the North. There were 12 first-class hotels, 40 restaurants, five hospitals, three theatres, four social clubs, four churches and more drinking and gambling establishments than you could count. And you could travel first-class all the way from Seattle to Dawson—the back-packing days were gone; it was trains and sternwheelers now.

Kate subtracted five years from her age and performed as a "teenage" dancer to the cheering bachelors of the town.

Picture the situation. Here were thousands of love-starved males, all far from home. Out in isolated creek valleys they worked in damp, cold, underground caverns. With other men as living companions they survived on rancid bacon, beans and the inevitable sourdough bread. They cooked, ate and slept in rough-built, crowded cabins and only washed up when they went to town. (Can you imagine the stink of it all?) When they did swagger into Dawson with their smoke-stained necks and grimy miners' clothes, they didn't have much appeal to women. Except for the gold they carried in their pokes.

Now comes Kate. She had a spectacular figure and knew how to show it off. One of her specialities might be called the Egyptian Number. Wrapped in a continuous bandage, she would spin around and around under the coloured spotlights until the bandage unravelled completely and she was left standing in her pink tights. If the Mounties weren't watching, a happy miner would hold one end of the bandage to start off her dance.

And sometimes she would come out on rollerskates or with a brace of lighted candles on her head. She could trail 50 yards of chiffon from a stick and, like an angel in pink tights, she undulated before the hungry eyes of the crowd.

Her voice was terrible. Something like gravel sluicing around in a tin rocker. But the rest of her more than made up for the lack of singing talent.

On Christmas Eve, 1900, some fellows gave her a crown. It was a tin can with the edges cut into sharp points and candles stuck onto it. They dubbed her the "Queen of the Klondike" at that all-night party and she hung onto that name for the rest of her life. The newspapers of the town continued to ignore her; the real stars such as Annie O'Brien and Beatrice Lorne took all the credits. Once in a while Kate Rockwell`s name appeared as part of a show cast.

She worked at the Palace Grand off and on and at most of the other theatres and dance halls of the town. And she made money. Besides her salary she sometimes made $500 a night in tips and bonuses. She bought a Paris gown worth $1500, a $250 plumed hat, studded with gold nuggets. (Not a belt, that was Cad Wilson who had that given to her a couple of years before.)

And then she fell in love. With a real shark. His name was Alexander Pantages, a short, swarthy Greek immigrant with one obsession: the piling up of money.

Pantages' first enterprise in Dawson was peddling coal oil from a hand drawn sleigh. He then became a bartender who kept his fingers sticky for weighing out gold dust from the drunken miners. The only people who liked him were the dance hall girls. He was cold-mannered, humourless—and mysterious; I guess that's what got to the women. Especially Kate.

They shacked up, Kate and Alex, and using her money bought the Orpheum Theatre. It quickly became very popular and of course, as the owner, Kate billed herself as the star.

Somewhere in this period Kate went south for a month. When she returned she had a brand new baby.

"I was taking care of a dying dance hall girl," she said, "and I went in to check on her just as she was having a baby. I delivered the child and adopted it, kept it for three years. I sent it out the States finally and even paid for its college education. I like to think of that child as my son."

This was Kate during an interview in 1944. Many people suspected the child was her own but no one knew for sure.

The Orpheum made money for a time, but the days of the dance halls in Dawson were coming to an end. Respectable women—wives,

shopkeepers, teachers and so forth—were making it hot for the saloon girls. The Orpheum's daily receipts went from $8,000 a day to practically being unable to cover expenses. Without some sleazy stage acts, charges for dancing, booze-peddling, gambling, and of course, the "touch-the-button girls" (these girls sat in a booth with a miner coaxing him to drink expensive champagne until he passed out) the dance halls were a lost cause for their owners. In 1901 Kate and Alex closed up shop and went south.

They returned after a couple of months and attempted to run the Orpheum using clean stage entertainment. But it didn't pay so they sold the theatre and left the Klondike behind them. Dawson itself was a dying town. For the miners the easy gold was gone—and so it was for the saloon keepers and "sporting women."

Kate said later that she and her lover had $150,000 when they left the Klondike. That figure is more likely to have been about $50,000. It was still a good sum of money in 1902.

So here was Kate Rockwell:

young, beautiful, in love, and rich. But for her, though she wouldn't have believed it at the time, the best days of her life were now behind her.

She went on tour in the States, sent all her money to Pantages who was starting a theatre chain. His new enterprise would grow into the biggest such business in North America. While Kate and Alex were separated, he married Lois Mendenhall, a classy young violin player.

Brokenhearted, absolutely brokenhearted was Kate. In this she did not lie because the rest of her life bears it out.

She took Pantages to court in a breach-of-promise suit and they awarded her $5000. Then she headed for the Klondike once more to recoup her fortunes. It was not to be.

Dawson already had a new star—Marjorie Rambeare—and after only four months Kate moved south again. She played in a few vaudeville troupes but her magic was gone. She bought a hotel in Fairbanks, Alaska (Swiftwater Bill's new town), but it burned down and she lost everything. She danced in some of the saloons there but poor Kate just couldn't turn the boys on. She went on another tour in the U.S. with Jimmy Ray. Finally, she quit show business and moved to Bend, Oregon.

In dingy cafes the Queen of the Klondike served meals to riffraff. Her behind was often pinched and sometimes she took a customer home. Once, in desperate straits, she went to see the famous Alex at his mansion and begged him for money. He gave her six dollars and sent her away. He did send her a few dollars a month after that to stay away from him. Drinking heavily now every chance she got, Kate spent the next twenty years in and around Bend, Oregon. A forgotten queen, to say the least.

The years went slowly by. In 1929 Alex Pantages' wife ran over two people with her car, killing them both; she was dead-drunk at the time. In the same month a young lady called Eunice Pyle laid criminal assault and statutory rape charges against the theatre big shot. The prosecution called in Kate Rockwell as a character witness against her former lover.

Her testimony wasn't required but the newspapers had a field day going over the wrongs Pantages had committed against Kate. Day after day, she sat in the courtroom, staring at the back of Pantages' head. Many former Klondikers rejoiced that the Greek would finally pay for his sins.

Pantages was found guilty and led away—amidst the great financial crash of 1929—to begin a fifty year sentence. At a new trial two years later, it was proven that the charges against him were false. His wife, in the meantime, had to pay $78,500 in damages for her accident. Pantages died suddenly in 1936 and it was rumoured during those years that he had been framed by a group of former Yukon sourdoughs: it was their revenge for the ruin he had brought to the "Golden Girl of the North."

Kate kept her name in the press. A great nostalgia for the Gold Rush years had come upon the aging Klondikers, 30,000 of whom had returned from there empty-handed and humbled by their adventure.

But now they remembered the good parts of it. And even the parts they didn't remember but sounded good were circulated among newspapers and magazines during the Depression years. Of course, this included the story of the "Queen of the Klondike," Kate Rockwell.

With every interview, Kate's story got better and better:

"Ah, yes, I was named the queen of it all! There were whistles and cheers whenever I appeared on the streets of Dawson; but I was never a gold digger. Jack London was there writing his stories and a girlfriend

Palace Grand theatre in 1961, prior to restoration. Kate's ghost is said to haunt one of the upstairs dressing rooms. [National Museum photo]

of mine was auctioned off for her weight in gold."

These things did happen in Dawson but not to Kate; she was simply giving her version of events that occurred during the Gold Rush of 1897-1898, which was over before she got there.

Around the time of the Pantages trial, one of the newspaper stories written about her made its way to a lonely cabin in the Yukon, sixty miles northwest of Dawson City. A grizzled old trapper and miner with Slavic features and a weather-lined face gazed at Kate's picture and read the story over and over. He was Johnny Matson, otherwise known as the Silent Swede.

With the help of a friend, he wrote a letter to Kate. In it he expressed the love he had held in his miner's heart for thirty lonesome years—ever since he had seen her twirling and laughing on the stage of the Orpheum back in 1901.

She answered his letter; he answered back. On July 14, 1933, Kate aged 52, and Johnny, 69, were married in Vancouver. He started a bank account in her name and left by himself for his gold claim and trapline. She came up to see him several times over the years and during these "honeymoon" visits they stayed in separate hotels in Dawson. She would walk by the old Orpheum Theatre, boarded up now, weather-blackened, nothing but silence within its leaning walls. The oldtimers of the town shook their heads and muttered to themselves: "There's that bitch again, back for more of Matson's gold."

The next few years were quite happy for Kate. Matson sent enough money for her to live on and she made many public appearances as Klondike Kate. In 1946, she received a last letter from the Silent Swede:

"My dearest wife, I am so tired after this trip."

The letter was unsigned. A concerned trapper and miner by the name of Joe Sestak went to investigate. He found some of Johnny Matson's bones: they had been scattered over a ten mile radius by bears and wolverines. Later, as he guided the Mounties to Matson's cabin, Sestak fell and gouged out an eye. He hired a young Yukon lawyer named Eric Nielsen to recover damages from the government and was finally awarded $3072.

Kate quickly sent word to Dawson that all Matson's possessions now belonged to her. She made a final journey to the Yukon to see what he had left her. It was a wasted trip. Apart from $1600 in a Vancouver bank, his cabin and gold claim were worthless. He had $30,000 when he wrote her that first letter.

Kate remarried in 1948 for a total of four marriages altogether. She died in February, 1957, at the age of 80.

Kate Rockwell symbolizes the Klondike Gold Rush quite well. While there certainly was a lot of gold in the creeks around Dawson, there wasn't as much as the newspapers said.

The whole episode rose and died like a giant flame, pulling the world out of hard times as it did so. To this day, Dawson City dwells on the glories of its past and makes money every year re-living it for the benefit of tourists.

Madame Tremblay

A young French Canadian woman hummed softly to herself as she prepared the evening meal in her mother's kitchen. Her mama's voice broke into Emilie Fortin's thoughts:

"Emilie! We have a guest coming for supper. From the north—Alaska, I think."

"Okay, mama. I'll make a little extra."

"Better make plenty extra," came her mother's voice again. "He's a very big man. Rough, too. You saw him back home in Quebec some years ago; you were only a child then. He left to go adventuring and is here only for a short visit. His name is Pierre-Nolasque Tremblay."

The family gathered round the big table. As the food was being trundled from the kitchen to the dining room, their guest arrived.

Now the females of the household stopped their chatter as they went about their work; and cast sly glances at the stranger. Even Mrs. Fortin could find nothing to say. For this young man, though he'd left Quebec as an innocent young lumberjack, had returned as something else: something wild, raw—but confident. It was as if he had brought the very spirit of that far-off land with him.

He sat down to eat, silent as the rest. His eyes followed the full figure of Emilie Fortin as she carried food from the kitchen and cleared

Emilie Tremblay

the table after each course. When she sat down he stared unashamedly at her pretty, dark-skinned features and she stared back with mischievous brown eyes. A message as old as time flashed between them in a silent rhythm...

When they finished the meal, the family asked this Nolasque

Tremblay to recount some of his adventures. He stood up, taking a small leather pouch from his vest pocket, loosening the top tie and then turned it upside down. A stream of gold nuggets clattered loudly onto the hard surface of the table, and sharp intakes of breath made the only other sound. They gaped at the gleaming treasure spread out before them. Everyone knew, though they had never seen it before, that this had to be gold. Not taking their eyes off it, they waited for the tall young Frenchman to speak.

Nolasque Tremblay, known as Jack Tremblay in the Yukon, had left his native province of Quebec at the age of 21. He eventually wandered west and then north into the valley of the Yukon River, arriving in that unknown land in 1886.

He fit right into the lifestyle there and soon gained a reputation as a true follower of the Code of the North. Ever ready to help a friend, generous, honest, physically tough—these were the traits of the whitemen wandering up and down the creeks and rivers of Alaska and the Yukon. All of them, including Jack, were looking for gold.

At this time the world was in the grip of economic recession, so $1,000 constituted a sizable fortune. Anyhow, it was only by chance that he wandered into Cohoes, New York, where he met his future bride. By now he was 33 years old.

He quickly proposed to Emilie Fortin, then 22, and she accepted. She knew she married both him and the land he talked about constantly, with so many a wave of his arm to the north. So, into the very heart of this unmapped, savage frontier, Emilie Tremblay accompanied her husband in the spring of 1894.

Leaving all her skeptical, perhaps envious friends and her tearful mother, Emilie left with Jack on the great adventure. Across the continent by train to Vancouver, then by ship to Juneau, Alaska went Jack and Emilie, arriving there on March 30th. They hired a small boat to take them up the Lynn Canal to Wilson Post. From there they walked along the Dyea trail to the

From the cabin on opposite page. A broken window stuffed with a pillow.

This is from the photo on the opposite page. What do you suppose is in the covered pail?

foot of the not-yet-famous Chilkoot Pass. Three wild-looking Chilkat Indian packers carried most of the gear.

The Tremblays didn't run into all the troubles that terrorized the greenhorns who came in later during the Gold Rush, but they did have some exciting moments. A few miles from Wilson Post, Jack turned back to retrieve some forgotten items, leaving his wife alone in the tent except for two dogs. A mountain blizzard blew in and Emilie awoke to find herself unable to move. She was completely covered with heavy, wet snow. She managed to free one arm and cut a hole in the side of the tent. The dogs freed themselves and went out through the opening. Their excited barking woke up the members of another travelling party who came over and shovelled Emilie out of her predicament.

Then they climbed the snow-covered Chilkoot Pass and slid on their backsides down the other side to the edge of Crater Lake. The following day they reached Lake Bennett and camped there for several weeks while Jack and his men built two boats. At last the ice broke up and they set out. They floated across a chain of lakes and short rivers until they came to the dreaded Miles Canyon and Whitehorse Rapids. Here Emilie got out and walked along the cliffs above the river while Jack and the others shot through the rapids with the boats.

They ate fish, greasy bear meat, porcupine, sea gull eggs berries—whatever the land provided. Emilie cooked with their meager utensils and at night they slept in a small tent on shore. At the time, she didn't fully realize the dangers of this 700-mile journey because her

Madame Tremblay on Miller Creek, 1895. She likely shaved her hair because the cabins in those days were infested with lice. Note the large-size gold pan, made for men with strong backs; also the wooden boxes by the door, likely used to classify gold-bearing gravels. (Yukon Archives photo #82/3 h-154, V. Wilson Collection)

husband Jack was so well-versed in the hazards of wilderness travel. For the newlyweds the whole trip was a delightful experience. In later years Emilie recalled her feelings:

"This first trip down the Yukon River remains in my memory full of romance, joy, and love. There was nothing like it in all the world."

At Fort Selkirk a native came upon Emilie sitting alone while her husband talked to the trader. The Indian sold her a fish then stayed by, staring at her wondrously. Jack came back and spoke to him in "Chinook." (Chinook was the universal language of the north, being a mixture of French, English and native languages—about 300 words in all.) The Indian wanted to know if Emilie was "Jack's little girl."

"No," said Jack. "She is my little wife."

They passed the mouth of the Klondike River—as yet only a landmark letting them know they had 50 miles to go. No one in the party could have envisioned the wild town that would spring up on that spot just two years later. The Tremblays arrived at Fortymile on June 16, 1894.

The town had a few saloons. A preacher and his wife lived there, and the rest of the inhabitants were eccentric bachelors or else they "lived in sin" with Indian women. Some of these ladies were greatly curious to see young Emilie, one of the first white women in that part of the country. She spoke of it in later years:

"Although they were friendly enough, I was apprehensive for they would touch me on the back, pull at my long skirt, and murmur among themselves. The next day they came again to admire me; they wouldn't sit down but stared curiously as if I were a caged animal."

Along with a couple of other miners and some native packers, the couple left for Miller Creek. They poled a boat up the Fortymile River as far as Moose Creek and from there they walked over the divide, down into the valley of Miller Creek. The whole trip was some 60 miles. Through swamp and muskeg, over cold mountain trails above the tree-line, and through fire-killed timber areas—where every step meant climbing over a fallen, char-black tree trunk—Emilie plodded along in her long skirts. Clouds of mosquitoes hovered constantly about their heads. At one point they became so thirsty they drank muddy water from a sink-hole pushed in by Emilie's foot. At last they came to the cabin—the home she had travelled 5000 miles to see. At that moment she could have turned and gone back over the tortuous trail; for she did not like what she saw:

"It was just a log cabin with a sod roof and a small aperture in one of the walls. And Jack said, 'Emilie, there is your home.'

"We went in. There was only one room with a pole in the middle supporting the roof. Bottles filtered the light through the little window. The floor was part log and part dirt and the cabin was repulsively dirty. The foot of the center pole was covered with a layer, deep and black. It was the miner's spittoon, Emilie's husband explained:

"You see, Emilie, when the miners are lying down on their bunks, tired and exhausted after the day's work, they don't take the trouble to get up and spit. They aim at the pole where they know they will not hit anyone."

Somehow Emilie cleaned up the cabin. Jack Tremblay felt himself to be the most fortunate man in all the Yukon; and every miner in the district came to admire his wife. Many of them predicted she would never stay.

But Jack and Emilie were very much in love. They teased each other gaily and ate their meals by candlelight, while outside the cabin the endless wilderness stretched out all around them. But still, it must have been a lonely time for the young bride. As yet she spoke only French and so could talk to no one but Jack.

In the spring of 1895, however, a Mr. and Mrs. Day and their children moved into the valley. Emilie visited them often and began to learn a bit of English. By the end of that summer Jack had mined enough gold to take them "outside" for a holiday. And a good thing it was that they were leaving. Their supplies had run so low by summer's end that they were eating beans three times a day.

On this trip they boarded a small sternwheeler which took them down the Yukon River to St. Michael, Alaska. From there a ship took them to Vancouver where they boarded a train for the East. Emilie, so happy to see her family again, had many stories to tell them. The Tremblays did not come back to the Yukon until the spring of 1898. Emilie's mother, who had always opposed her daughter's desire to return to the Yukon, died suddenly, and the couple made plans to head north again. But now things would

go differently, because in 1898 the Klondike Gold Rush had reached its most feverish stage.

As Jack and Emilie came over the mountain passes again, they witnessed the terrible snowslide that killed 74 people. Emilie's cousin, travelling with them, died at Lake Bennett and two other relatives became very sick. Such was the Trail of '98. It had been much easier the first time, when they had the whole route to themselves. Now it was clogged with thousands of goldseekers, all frantic to reach Dawson City.

Using their wilderness experience, the Tremblays reached the Klondike without mishap; but like

Madame Tremblay at a cabin on Bonanza Creek.

everyone else, they were too late to stake a rich claim. All the dry goods they had brought in to sell turned out to be almost worthless; thousands of disillusioned stampeders were selling their outfits for next to nothing. And their Miller Creek property had been considered abandoned and taken over by others.

For the next 15 years Jack Tremblay worked for wages on the rich creeks around Dawson. When he had the time and money, he prospected for gold but never did find a good spot. He later bought some claims on Bonanza Creek and mined there for several years, barely making expenses. In l906 he hit a rich pocket, one the previous owners had missed, and that year he and Emilie went on a trip to Europe. They travelled first-class and in France they stayed with a wealthy Klondiker who had bought a huge castle with his gold. The Tremblays even visited the Pope in Rome. On her return Madame Tremblay, as folks called her now, was to say she preferred the miners of Dawson to the high society of Europe.

In 1913 she opened her famous shop in the downstairs of their home at the corner of Third and King Street in Dawson. The building and her sign are still there, now restored to original condition by Parks Canada. She ran the store for 30 years. Contrary to legend, she brought only one shipment of gowns and exotic perfumes from Paris; after that the store mainly carried ladies' wear and novelties.

Jack Tremblay died in l935, having earned the title of Grand Old Man of the Yukon.

Madame Tremblay took part in many social activities in Dawson. She formed the society of the Ladies of the Golden North; was a member of the Imperial Order of the Daughters of the Empire; and in l937 she received a commemorative medal of the coronation of King George VI.

In l940, she married another miner, Louis Lagrois. She closed her store and with her new husband lived in a cabin at the junction of Bonanza and Eldorado Creeks (Grand Forks). When Emilie turned 75 and Louis 80, they moved to a boarding house in Victoria, B. C. She died of cancer in l949 and Louis passed away in l956.

Madame Tremblay had let it be known that she was the first white woman to cross the Chilkoot Pass and she became widely celebrated for this. However, a Mrs. Beaumont crossed the Pass in l892 and went on to Fortymile. Before that, "sporting women," as they were called, came in over the same route on their way to the new mining camps.

But it can be said that Madame Tremblay was one of the first white women to settle in the Yukon. She was greatly loved by the miners, performed many good works in her life, especially for the sick. Only age and poor health could have induced her to leave her adopted land. In Whitehorse they've named a school after her and of course her old store in Dawson is now a tourist attraction. Her story is one of romance and courage and a kind of downright goodness; and you could say she lived a rich, interesting life here in the Yukon.

Christmas on Miller Creek, 1894
By Madame Tremblay

"As I was the only woman at Miller Creek during that winter of 1894-95, I decided, with my husband, to invite all the miners and prospectors living in the neighborhood for Christmas. They were about a dozen.

"All our winter's supplies had been brought in by Jack and his men on their backs. Those supplies therefore were limited. As for the kitchen utensils, we had only the minimum: two plates, two spoons, two forks, and two knives.

"We had plenty of meat. Caribou was plentiful and the jackrabbits abounded in the valley. The meat question was settled although we had not enough dishes to serve it.

"As for vegetables, I would prepare a big pot of beans and for dessert I could have a prune pudding.

"Using some birch bark for paper, I sent an invitation to all miners to attend our supper on Christmas Day at 6:00 p.m. At the bottom of the invitation I added: 'Bring your own spoon, fork and knife.'

"The biggest problem for me was to cook enough meat for all those men. My stove measured only 22" x 22" and in the narrow oven I could place a pan only six inches wide.

"It was not a question of money—we had plenty of it—but of transport. How could you bring a big stove over the mountains to a place like Miller Creek?" And here is the menu of that famous dinner shared by 12 men:

Stuffed Rabbits...Roast of Caribou
Brown Beans au Bacon
King Oscar Sardines
Evaporated Potatoes
Butter and Sourdough Bread
Prune Pudding
Cake

"The pudding was made of dried prunes with a blueberry sauce. We had to use powdered eggs instead of fresh eggs.

"In my wardrobe I took one of those long skirts whose use was then fashionable, a skirt I had never worn, and cut it up and used it as a tablecloth.

"One prospector was missing when all our guests had arrived at the cabin. Some said he had been gone for three days. We sat down to dinner. At the end of the meal who should arrive but the missing guest who put a bottle of rum on the table. He had walked 30 miles in the snow to go and get that bottle and had walked 30 miles back to bring it to us and enhance our little celebration.

"After dinner we played cards and I gave the miners permission to smoke. They all hastened to fill up their pipes for there were no cigarettes in those days. And they smoked so much that the whole cabin was filled with blue smoke.

"Happy to have spent such a nice Christmas dinner and evening together. All the miners went home late, taking with them their own utensils..."

Dawson City Post Office in 1961. Built in 1901, it has been restored by Parks Canada. [National Film Board photo]

Robert Service and
Destiny

Did you ever know someone with the Midas touch? Whose every enterprise turns over a profit and it seems they were born to succeed? Or, a carpenter who whistles while he works? And what about the great military commanders for whom a war just happens to come along?

Robert Service, the Yukon's most famous poet, would have described these men as being in harmony with their Fate—with Destiny.

Destiny doesn't just arrive in a person's life; no, it often must be sought after and prepared for. It doesn't come to the *"stagnant ones"* but only to those who embark on a moving quest. The trick is to step out of the mold, away from security and comfort, and let Fate take a hand. But alas to those who misread Her signs or forget the limits of their given strength: to them comes calamity or merciful death.

Bob Service thought a lot about these things and spent a lifetime expressing the laws of Fate through his stories and ballads and poems. To him, his own life was a fair example of a man being *"guided and pushed by the gods."*

Robert W. Service was born on January 16, 1874, in Lancashire, England. His family of seven boys, three girls and parents, moved from there to Glasgow, Scotland. Robert was sent to live with his grandfather and three old maid aunts. After several years he again lived with his large family in Glasgow. In his own words he was *"exhibitionist, impertinent,"* and loved reading romantic stories of adventure and travel.

At the age of 15 he apprenticed to the Bank of Scotland. His father was immensely pleased with this and Robert stayed with the bank for six years. He continued to read, especially poetry, and published numerous articles in Glasgow magazines.

In 1896 he departed for Canada with his mind set on becoming a prairie settler or a cowboy. On Vancouver Island he dug potatoes on a farm for a while then hired on as a cowboy on a big ranch. The glory of it soon wore off in spite of his ability to quick draw a gun from a holster; and in low spirits he drifted to San Francisco.

He loafed around there till his money ran out then took a job as a tunneller in the San Gabriel Canyon. *"Excruciating, mindless toil"* it was; and he quit upon receiving his first cheque. He had to sell it for half its value lest he starve before reaching a bank, and with that money spent he was again *"just another bum to be treated like a dog."*

He rode a train to Los Angeles where he lived in a mission house with vagrants, alcoholics and down and outers of all description. Lying on his bunk, reading books from the nearby library, he pondered how he would go *"forward to whatever destiny awaited him."* Half starved now, he went picking oranges for as long as he could stand it and hit upon the idea of advertising his talents in a newspaper.

As a result of the ad he was offered a job as tutor to three girls in a mansion in San Diego. He soon learned he was temporarily replacing a black handyman and that the place was a high class brothel. The black man eventually returned and Robert was sent on his way with a gift from one of the whores: a Spanish guitar in a brown leather case.

To Mexico, then north again to Los Angeles wandered the future poet. In a hut made of railroad ties he met a robber and killer, and to get away from the man he slept in a ground hollow full of dead leaves. About this time he met another young Scotsman with the name of Service; and he felt ashamed even to meet the man's family.

"Then something seemed to twist me right around, and bidding good bye, I went off in the opposite direction...what was directing my steps? Well, a force stronger than myself seemed to be drawing me on to another destiny, and even though it looked a gloomy one, I must fulfil it."

In great despair he hunched on a park bench, wondering just what to do. Although just 23 years old, he had had a belly full of physical labour. He began to think about working in an office again. In the meantime, a man sitting beside him on the bench left behind a newspaper. The paper, which Robert quickly salvaged, described the Great Klondike Gold Rush in glowing terms. One sentence leaped from the page; and it spelled out ever so clearly what Fate had decreed for him, this bum sitting alone in a park:

"No doubt another Bret Harte will arise and sing of it (The Gold Rush) in colourful verse."

But still he didn't go north to the Great Alone.

Through Colorado, Arizona, Nevada, all over the West he roamed, losing his beloved guitar along the way. After a short, disastrous stint in a sawmill he boarded a ship for British Columbia, again after reading a newspaper left on a park bench.

On the same ranch where he had worked before, he herded wild cattle. That winter of 1899-1900, a ferocious bull knocked him down, breaking a few of his ribs. As he lay in pain and despair, he *"cursed the gods who were laughing at my fate."* But perhaps Fate had just nudged him forward, this time more forcefully than Robert would have liked.

The storekeeper on the ranch had quit and Robert took over the job. Once more he was *"a white collar man...a bourgeois."* With his meals prepared by the boss's wife and with time for reading, fishing and socializing, he eased along this way until 1903. But he knew he was wasting his time, that Fate had something more meaningful in store, and one day it was time to move along.

He would become a schoolteacher. After intense studying, he flunked the entrance exams to the teaching college. Buying some respectable clothes, he applied for clerical jobs with no result. One afternoon he met an old friend, a biscuit salesman, and they stood talking in front of the Canadian Bank of Commerce in Victoria, B.C.

"Why don't you try for a job in this bank?" said the friend. Wearing his good clothes and holding forth his letter of recommendation from the Bank of Scotland, Robert went in to see the manager and was hired.

"On what accidents do our destinies depend!" he wrote later. *"How we are at the mercy of the insignificant!"*

He worked for the bank at Victoria and at Kamloops, B.C. On November 8, 1904, they transferred him to Whitehorse, Yukon Territory. In stark contrast to the Argonauts of 1897-98, Robert rode into the Yukon by steamship and train.

Dawson City was the capital of the Yukon then; but Whitehorse, by virtue of its location at the end of the White Pass & Yukon Railway and the start of navigation on the Yukon River, was truly a place where all Yukoners met. For the next two years Robert socialized— although he was very shy and awkward—and listened to tales of adventure and hardship. He enjoyed walking alone over the trails leading to Miles Canyon and other scenic spots. He *"felt poetry all around him"* and, with verses ringing in his mind, it was only a matter of time until he set them down on paper.

In 1906 he wrote a poem for a church concert. It was called *"The Shooting of Dan McGrew."* He wasn't allowed to read it in church; in fact, it was too rough even for the Whitehorse Star so Robert stuck it in a bureau drawer and continued writing other ballads.

Into the drawer went *The Cremation of Sam McGee, The Call of the Wild, The Spell of the Yukon, The Parson's Son,* and many more. He walked his lonely walks and the words poured into his mind as if the Spirit of the Yukon had selected him to be her personal scribe:

"There's a land where the mountains are nameless,
And the rivers all run God knows where;
There are lives that are erring and aimless,
And deaths that just hang by a hair..."

(From The Spell of the Yukon)
"Wild and wide are my borders, stern as death is my sway,
   And I wait for the men who will win me—and I will not be won in a day..."
(From The Law of the Yukon)

"I'm one of the Arctic brotherhood, I'm an old-time pioneer.
   I came with the first—O God! how I've cursed this Yukon—but I'm still here..."
(From The Parson's Son)

"Were you ever out in the Great Alone, when the moon was awful clear,
   And the icy mountains hemmed you in with a silence you most could hear..."
(From The Shooting of Dan McGrew)

So, before he ever reached the goldfields of the Klondike (and this is the miracle of it!), Robert Service became the voice of the Yukon prospector. His stories rang with the authenticity of personal experience. If ever an author was spoken to by muses, it was he. Almost entirely self-taught, he described the land and its inhabitants—how they felt— in soul-catching verse. And, even more than Jack London, he created the mystique of the North.

The story of "Dangerous Dan and The lady that's known as Lou" could not have happened in the Yukon; the Mounties didn't allow six-guns in the bars, so Robert drew this plot from the American West. But even so, he tuned in to the Yukon experience and turned his understanding of it into a music of words.

His Destiny was fast closing in. He sent the poems to his father, who had emigrated to Toronto, and asked him to find a printing house so they could make it into a booklet. He enclosed a cheque to cover the costs and intended to give these booklets away to his friends in Whitehorse. Who should the senior Service take these ribald stories to but a publisher of Methodist hymn books. The employees of the print shop, supposedly devout Christians and used to proof-reading pious entreaties to God, saw in Robert's verses all the life and sinning so lacking in their own staid lives. And they loved them, went crazy over them!

The foreman and printers recited the ballads while they worked. A salesman read the proofs out loud as they came off the typesetting machines. Orders for 1700 copies of *Songs of A Sourdough* came in just by word of mouth.

The publisher, Briggs, sent Robert's cheque back to him and offered a ten percent royalty contract for the book. When that was signed, the book went into seven printings before it even officially came out; and a U.S. publisher quickly arranged for American printing rights.

In 1907, especially in Canada, Robert's ribald verses went against all literary trends. Any other publisher might have turned it down. But Briggs, because his employees had already sold many books, had a best-seller on his hands. He couldn't stop it if he wanted to.

When copies of the book reached Whitehorse, Robert's own minister took him aside to let him know how wicked were his stories,. Service hung his head in shame and regretted his writings ever going into print.

But, that summer, tourists from the south arrived in Whitehorse looking for the famous poet; and he autographed many of his books.

In April, 1908, he was transferred to the great Mecca of the North, Dawson City. Again, he didn't ask; he was sent. At last he made it to where it all had happened. And, on the same winter stage (actually, an open sleigh) on which he had been a passenger, a royalty cheque for one thousand dollars went through the mail. But still he wasn't happy.

Fast slipping into decline, Dawson City had only four thousand people left; many of these were company men and business folk. However, wandering the streets—now lined with empty saloons and boarded-up houses—were grizzled veterans of the Great Stampede. Out on the creeks lonely men still toiled underground and hiked into town with heavy pokes of gold. These men—and a few women—remembered the glory days with wistful pride. They could look back on their hardships and the whole panorama of the Gold Rush with an accuracy not possible during its happening. Then, it had been every man and woman for themselves and everyone thought the madness would go on forever.

So they talked, these veterans of the Stampede; they loved to reminisce, and Robert listened carefully and remembered. He wrote another book of verses, *Ballads of a Cheechako,* and, in the fall of 1908, sent it off to the same publisher.

It too was an overwhelming success. Even if he should never write another verse, these first two books would cinch his title as the best-paid poet of all time.

For the next two years he wrote nothing. He worked in the bank and hung around the sourdoughs and roughnecks of the town. He refused so many invitations to the high-class social events that they stopped inviting him. When distinguished visitors to Dawson asked for him he was rounded up and only then, reluctantly, would he attend one of these gatherings of the town's better citizens.

He poked around the boarded-up dance halls and saloons, went for solitary walks along the Yukon River, attended hangings or unusual events, and wooed a young stenographer without success. Her parents couldn't separate the writer from his stories; they believed, as did many, that Robert was telling tales on himself. In general he was known to be an oddball—a misfit who could do as he liked because of his fame and ever-increasing royalty cheques. He toyed with the idea of writing a novel but wasn't sure if he could do it; he had so far only written poetry, and prose might not be his line.

In 1909 the bank told him he was to take up the manager's position at the bank in Whitehorse. Now he was faced with deciding on a career with the bank or to continue writing. The fact that he had ten thousand dollars saved up from wages and royalties greatly influenced his decision to turn down the job! So now he turned his future over to his talents and, if you will, to Destiny.

Having quit the bank, he rented a cosy cabin in Dawson and went to work on his novel. Tacking up rolls of wallpaper, he wrote with a carpenter's pencil and stood back to examine his words. He went for walks that lasted all night, slept till mid-afternoon, and sometimes didn't come out of the cabin for days. In five months the novel, called *The Trail of '98*, was complete and he took it to a publisher in New York. It immediately became a best-seller.

After a year wandering around the U.S. and down to Cuba he came back to the Yukon—the hard way this time. He retraced the Edmonton Trail from Edmonton to Dawson and it was almost as difficult for him as it had been for the gold seekers of 1897-98. The **Dawson Daily News** gives a description of him when he finally arrived home:

"Our poet is back, with a face ambushed in an ebony thicket of three weeks growth, nose broiled to lobster red, hands a Mongolian shade, trousers shredded."

After all his writing about the tortuous trails, he had gone over one himself—and found himself equal to the job. This trip helped cancel the guilt he had always felt about his writing: that he was an impostor who lived only through the experience of other men.

Back in his beloved cabin he wrote another best-seller, *Rhymes of A Rolling Stone*. None of these later works came to him so easily as did his first book of ballads. Now he sweated over each verse, wresting them from his mind. Using rolls of wallpaper again and a large pencil, he would stand in the cabin and look at his lines on the wall, pace back and forth, change a word or two, go for walks or rides on his bicycle, come back to look at the wallpaper, and so forth. Each ballad came out carefully crafted but without the

magic of Dan McGrew or Sam McGee or The Parson's Son. However, they were excellent works and he always thought of them as being better than the ones which had made him famous.

In the fall of 1912 he boarded the last steamboat of the season out of Dawson City—and never returned.

He went on to become a war correspondent, a first aid man and ambulance driver during **World War One;** wrote more best selling poetry; became a husband and the master of a beautiful mansion in France. He travelled to Hollywood for work on a movie—all at his own leisurely pace while the royalties from his books kept him well supplied with money.

Altogether he wrote 14 books of poetry, six novels, a health book, and two autobiographies. He died in 1958 at the age of 84. Always humble about his talents, often embarrassed by his great success, perhaps these few lines from one of his poems might tell us what he thought about Fate and its role in life:

"Since plain within the Book of Destiny
Is written all the journey of mankind
Inexorably to the end; since blind
And mortal puppets playing parts are we:"

On a final note, one other word often replaces "Destiny" and "Fate" throughout the stories and poems of Robert W. Service: that word is...**God.**

Jack London's
Yukon Odyssey

Jack London

In the late fall of 1897, at the confluence of the Stewart and Yukon rivers, a group of men huddled in tiny cabins—some in tents—to wait for spring. For many of them it was to be the most terrible, wasted winter of their lives. In their confinement, locked in as they were by the unforgiving Yukon winter, they revealed their every experience to each other. And, whether wanting to or not, they also revealed their very souls. Each man had not a strength nor a weakness, not a defect of character nor an unrealized strength, that was not seen by the others. *One man who saw—and who remembered every detail—was Jack London.*

He would become the highest paid writer in the world; many of his books are still in print today and enjoy a worldwide audience. But, if it were not for the Klondike Gold Rush and his experiences in the Yukon, he might have lived and died as a complete unknown—and a dismal failure besides.

He was a tough little character of twenty-one when, with his partners, he packed his gear over the Chilkoot Pass in August, 1897. Although it was a feat to be proud of, he and his group made it through to the interior with less difficulty than thousands of others who were not so physically fit nor so inured to hardship. Because Jack was very skilful with small boats, he and his partners floated down the long chain of lakes and rivers into the Klondike without mishap. After piloting their own boats through the notorious Miles Canyon, Jack went back and ran another boat through as a favour to another party of goldseekers. So far on this trip he had witnessed the carnage of the Dead Horse Trail, had seen men and women completely paralyzed by despair. On Lake Bennett's Windy Arm he had watched helplessly while two boatloads of people capsized and drowned, their pitiful cries carried away by the wind and driving snow.

Any would-be writer must have good powers of observation. Jack quickly fathomed that the whole phenomenon of the Gold Rush was a farce. Only with some incredible luck would the expedition pay off. When he and his partners reached the mouth of the Stewart River they decided to camp there for the winter. It was still 80 miles down the Yukon River to Dawson City where people were known to be starving and paying exorbitant rents for any kind of shelter.

Young Jack London up to that time had thought of himself as the epitome of nineteenth century manhood. He had been a small-scale pirate, lover, tramp, sailor, and could hold his own—for short periods—on any job requiring brawn and fortitude. Because of his self-teaching and some brief flings at high school and university, he believed himself to be intellectually superior to almost everyone he met. The trip over the Chilkoot and down the Yukon River system, though fraught with danger, had been a lark for him. He looked condescendingly—and with some amount of pity—at the many who were overcome and who fell by the wayside or returned to their homes in the south.

But in the end the Yukon would break him and make him realize the one great fact about his life.

Before he joined the Gold Rush he had indeed lived a tumultuous life: a life dictated by circumstances and by his peculiar inability to withstand drudgery or routine for any great length of time.

He was born in San Francisco on January 12, 1876, into the tough economic times of the post-Civil War era. His real father, who later denied his paternity, escaped from Jack's mother, Flora. She then married a kindly, older man called John London.

The couple could never quite make ends meet. Flora was a flighty, ambitious, homely, domineering woman, involved with supernaturalism. Her instability caused the family fortunes—and locations—to change frequently, often

for the worse. Most of the time they lived in the Oakland area of California.

Jack ran two paper routes, picked up odd jobs, and gave the money to his mother. His favourite childhood recollections were to be of his dog, Rollo, and of his carefree trips around San Francisco Bay in his small rowboat and later a fourteen foot skiff. Later in life he liked to talk about the poverty of his youth; but when he was a teenager the family's black maid was able to loan him 300 dollars so he could buy a much-coveted boat. His skill with such boats would later prove invaluable in the Klondike.

He graduated from grammar school at the age of 14 and for the next four years, although he worked occasionally, Jack lived the life of a young hooligan. He drank in the waterfront bars, took a mistress when he was 16, and prided himself on being the *"King of the Oyster Pirates."* This was a group of youngsters engaged in stealing oysters from the beds belonging to a big company in San Francisco Bay. He called his boat the "Razzle Dazzle" and outwardly revelled in the roughness of his life style.

About this time his inner self—a finer, gentler self—betrayed him, as it would many times in his life: he tried to drown himself while drunk. A Greek fisherman pulled him out just in time.

Changing hats, he chased down his former friends while working for the Fish Patrol. Despite the excitement of life on the waterfront he could see the ultimate hopelessness of it all. He signed on as an ablebodied seaman on a sealing ship.

A Life of Drudgery

Returning to land eight months later, he entered an electrician's training program only to discover that the job consisted of shovelling coal into a boiler for sixteen hours a day. He couldn't take the drudgery, the "mindless toil," nor the lousy pay.

He hit the "Road" and with other groups of unemployed men he hoboed his way across the U.S.A. to New York; went from there to Ottawa, Canada, and hopped freight trains to Vancouver. From there he earned passage on a freighter to his mother's home in Oakland. During these wanderings he had languished for a month in a brutal prison, had witnessed tramp society with all its cruelties, and had come to view the economic system as being very unjust.

It was from these experiences that he began to form the socialistic ideas with which he struggled for the rest of his life. He never let them go, in spite of becoming rich himself. His books are still popular in the Soviet Union because of his railing against the capitalist system. Although he sympathized with the have-nots of his generation, he had no intention of staying down along with them, the "work beasts of society." It was around this period in his life that he decided to become a writer.

In 1893, at the age of 17, he wrote an article about a typhoon he experienced while aboard the sealing vessel. It won first prize in a writing contest and became his first published article. Two years later, after returning from his adventures on the "road," he entered the Oakland High School where he completed one year. He decided he was learning more in the public library than in school so he quit in the spring of 1896. By intense studying at home he passed the entrance exams to the University of California.

He was already familiar with the great writers of his day such as Spencer, Darwin, Kipling, Stevenson and others. His rough experiences had given him a differ-

The famous Miles Canyon.

ent outlook on life from his fellow students and he felt himself to be an outsider. He completed all the subjects of his first semester except English. In the spring of 1896 he dropped out of school again, citing financial difficulties.

He taught himself how to type, published two articles, and wrote feverishly. He could not make enough money to keep going. In despair he took a job in a steam laundry—an exhausting, tedious job which left him no time to read his beloved books.

He lasted three months and gave up in disgust. His heart was set on becoming a writer—a paid writer—but how was it to happen?

Around this time the news of a new gold field—a fabulous treasure trove—burst upon the world. The Klondike Gold Rush was about to begin.

A week after he heard the news, Jack headed north, grubstaked by his sister, Eliza.

Escape To Freedom

In the highest of spirits he started out with the first wave of goldseekers to head for the fabulous Klondike. Having escaped once more from the "fate of the work-beasts," he soon found himself labouring up the Chilkoot Pass like a

Goldseekers climbing the Chilkoot Pass

pack animal. With his friends, Jim Goodman, J.M. Sloper, F.C. Thompson and a new man called Tarwater (who Jack would later use as a character in his books, name and all) they made it as far as the mouth of the Stewart River. Ice was already floating into the Yukon River from the tributaries. A food shortage was predicted for Dawson, and they had heard that all the good claims had been staked. They decided to headquarter where they were and see what turned up.

They took possession of a cabin on Split-Up Island, so named because many parties broke up there—some even sawed their boats in half in order to divide their goods equally. Just the fact that Jack and his partners were not fighting was rather extraordinary compared with most of the other outfits on the long trail.

They went up Henderson Creek, which flowed into the Yukon River about four miles downstream from their cabin, and staked eight claims. A few colours turned up but the ground looked very disappointing compared with the stories they heard about the creeks around Dawson. They didn't know much about prospecting to start with and gave up on the idea rather quickly. Too quickly, for, in later years, the same ground yielded a considerable amount of gold to a dredging company.

(By September, 1898, some 17,000 claims had been staked in the Yukon. Most of them contained not enough gold to cover the recording fees.)

On October 16, 1897, Jack and his partners floated down to Dawson for a look at the town.

The City of Gold

The streets had been churned into muddy trails; the buildings had been slapped up with logs or rough-sawed lumber—some were half tent, half cabin—and some folks crouched under canvas lean-to's. A cold, wet fog rolled in from the river and clung to the mud and muskeg between the shanties and cabins. Along Front Street, which paralleled the river, music and laughter rang out all along the avenue. The M & N Dancehall, the Eldorado, the Moosehorn, the Monte Carlo, and a half-dozen other saloons took up the prime building space of the town.

All along the beach, boats and rafts had been tied to shore or to one another, with more coming in every day. Altogether, 5000 restless men paced the streets and bars, complaining about the shortage of food and about everything else in this godforsaken country. Many were already selling their outfits and pulling out. The biggest part of the rush was yet to come.

Jack London loitered about in Dawson for six weeks. He camped beside Louis Bond's cabin on the shoreline. Bond's half-Saint Bernard dog would become the hero in Jack's most famous novel—*The Call of the Wild.*

He had no trouble fitting in with this crowd. Everyone who recollected him said he was always in conversation with someone. His yellow hair had grown long and shaggy; he had a tooth missing from the front of his mouth. With his generally slovenly appearance, no one could have predicted how famous this gabby, friendly kid would be someday.

Conversation was the chief activity of Dawson. Although the saloons and dancehalls provided shows, booze, gambling and girls to dance with—at a dollar a dance—the cheechakos and sourdoughs gabbed and gossiped incessantly. Their favourite topics were the life histories of the Klondike Kings who threw their wealth around with reckless abandon—while the poor cheechakos stood by in wistful envy.

Candles and kerosene were in such short supply during the winter of 1897-98 that the brightly lit honkytonks offered the only alternative to sitting in a dark, drafty cabin. In the streets men moved silently, muffled up against the biting cold as they trudged from one saloon to another. Besides the crunching of feet on the crystallized snow, the only other outdoor sound came from hundreds of dogs.

They barked constantly or, in the case of malamutes, howled mournfully, pausing only to listen for an answering call from another husky across town.

Most of the cheechakos were broke. As they watched the endless quantities of gold being squandered, they thought about the day they must leave—broker than when they had arrived. Too, many of the stampeders had borrowed from friends and family to finance their trip. This heightened their shame and regret at having come so far only to find that the gone was gone and they must leave empty handed.

In desperation they went on wild stampedes at the merest hint of a new gold strike somewhere.

They drooled over the sexy dance hall queens whose sultry smiles were aimed at the men with the heaviest gold pokes.

Some of the men from the creeks, such as Swiftwater Bill Gates or Nigger Jim Dougherty, bathed and shaved and then dressed in the finest clothes that could be had in the embryo town. It was a town in which food and medical attention were almost unobtainable but which fairly overflowed with whisky and gold.

But most men only had one set of clothes, their skin had been darkened from sun and woodsmoke, and to bathe frequently was to invite respiratory diseases or worse. Their diet of beans, rancid bacon and sourdough bread—besides giving rise to scurvy—caused such flatulence among the men that the

Lulu, a dancehall girl from the days of the Gold Rush.

breaking of wind was as common as belching or uttering a sigh of discontent. The oldtimers in the country did not notice the smell at all and the newcomers—cheechakos— soon became accustomed to the Yukon air: cold, clear and sweet outside; but in the cabins and saloons, hot, smoky, thick with the odour of whisky, tobacco, and unwashed, uncaring men. The women wore the heaviest of perfumes—heavy enough to generate waves of femininity as they swished around the sawdust covered floors of the honkytonks in their long, brightly coloured gowns.

It was a masculine environment, one that suited Jack London very well.

He was seen talking at the bar to Swiftwater Bill, to Big Alex Macdonald-the King of the Klondike—and to anyone with an interesting story to tell. Jack listened so intently, could talk so intelligently on so many subjects, that he was able to rub shoulders with the elite of the town, rough and tumble though they were. In later years the eccentric prospectors and wild miners would be shunned by the civilized folk that came into the country afterward. But for now these men were the undisputed Kings of Eldorado. At this time too, most of the women were as rough in their own way as the men, no matter how much they tried to look and act like ladies.

In his books about the Klondike, Jack London would always ignore the obvious prostitution of Dawson. His fictional heroines would invariably be beautiful, tender hearted females whose troubles were caused entirely by men.

Had Jack arrived during the later rush of 1898, he would not have had the chance to meet such a diversity of characters as he did during his six weeks in Dawson in the fall of 1897. Although he made one trip out to Bonanza Creek, it is clear that he spent most of his time in the saloons. Talking, arguing, listening, observing. Although scurvy was already affecting his body and inwardly he knew the whole trip was a bust, he smiled and joked with all those about him. He didn't try for a labouring job out in the mines .

A dancehall queen called Little Egypt.

On Thanksgiving Day, 1897, a dancehall girl named Belle Mitchell threw a lighted lamp at a rival and the resulting fire burned half of Dawson's businesses to the ground. The same woman, a year later, left a candle burning in a block of wood while she visited some prostitutes across the river in Lousetown. During her absence the town went up in flames again. This fire and other events the young Jack London witnessed during his sojourn in Dawson would provide him with a colourful background for his future stories. Perhaps only a battlefield could have contained such human trauma and action as did the City of Gold during that first year of the Klondike Gold Rush.

Return to Split-Up Island

On December 3, Jack and his friends left Dawson to go over the Yukon River ice to their winter quarters on Split-Up Island. It would be there, in a terrible confinement lasting five more months, that he would come to know himself and in so doing would come to know the hearts and minds of men that were worse—or better—than he.

On November 29, 1897, Dawson City recorded a temperature of 67 below zero Fahrenheit. At that temperature all movement, animal or human, becomes an agony. Deep breathing brings a searing pain into the lungs and even inanimate objects shrivel and harden into a fragile bitterness. Trees crack like gunshots at the slightest swaying of their tops and snow turns into a dry, sugar-like sand into which the feet plunge to the solid ground beneath. Animals

crawl into their dens or huddle together, sensibly, conserving their strength and body heat. Even a mighty force like the Yukon River slows up, the creeks feeding into it frozen to their very bottoms. A cap of ice, hard as steel and able to bear many tons of weight, forms on the river surface; and it once again becomes a highway for those who must travel.

Jack and F.C. Thompson set out from Dawson during the worst of the cold snap. They travelled in the few hours of daylight and in the dark to make their twenty miles a day.

They crawled over stretches of pack ice and tried to stay on the trail which followed the inside bends of the river, where the ice was safest. To miss the trail by a foot meant a waist-deep plunge into the snow. They dozed at night by a roaring fire, taking turns to feed it while the other slept. On the fourth day they reached the settlement at Split-Up Island. They stumbled into the warm cabin they shared with two other men and did not leave it till the temperature rose to a more seasonable forty below.

Had each man, of the 80 or so that languished in the haphazard grouping of cabins and tents, been able to spend much time alone he might have seriously contemplated suicide. For this was the final folly—to be cooped up on a group of tiny islands, frozen in for the coming months, under the realization that all the terrible privations and adventures of getting into the Yukon had been in vain. They had been hoodwinked, although no one cared to openly admit it. The majority of them had entirely given up on the notion of finding great riches in this lonely, frozen country. Jack London, however, did not surrender so easily as the others.

But, again, he found himself working at slave labour; this time for no pay at all.

A determined group of men, perhaps a dozen, were burning holes down to bedrock in a fruitless attempt to discover a paystreak on the right fork of Henderson Creek. This process, which involves melting the frozen muck and gravel with firewood then scooping off the melted layer before setting the fire again, is a painfully slow, laborious task. Even more so if no gold is found at the bottom. The goldseekers on this particular stretch of ground saw just enough colour to encourage further efforts—until finally they gave up in disgust.

The cabin (part of it) Jack stayed in while on Henderson Creek now rests at Dawson City as a tourist attraction.

The men he worked with there, and those in the camp at Split-Up, would almost all become characters in his fictional writings about the Klondike. The cold weather hikes over narrow trails, life in a tiny cabin, dog teams passing by the settlement, cabin fever (nowadays called "seasonal affective disorder"), death, the many acts of heroisim—these were the legacies of the Yukon to Jack London. One day he would use every memory in his retentive mind to produce one of the finest bodies of literature to come out of the Klondike Gold Rush period.

But he had to suffer for some time yet, both in and out of the Yukon.

Through all he kept a cheerful countenance and except for a row

Jack London's cabin, part of which was moved to Dawson City, largely because of the efforts of author Dick North.

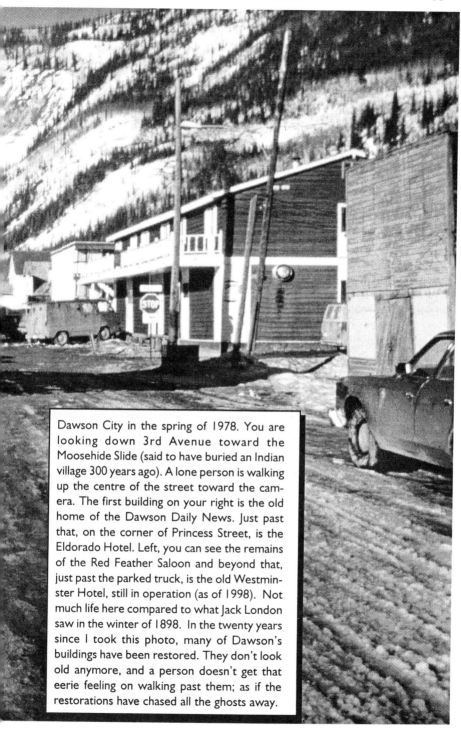

Dawson City in the spring of 1978. You are looking down 3rd Avenue toward the Moosehide Slide (said to have buried an Indian village 300 years ago). A lone person is walking up the centre of the street toward the camera. The first building on your right is the old home of the Dawson Daily News. Just past that, on the corner of Princess Street, is the Eldorado Hotel. Left, you can see the remains of the Red Feather Saloon and beyond that, just past the parked truck, is the old Westminster Hotel, still in operation (as of 1998). Not much life here compared to what Jack London saw in the winter of 1898. In the twenty years since I took this photo, many of Dawson's buildings have been restored. They don't look old anymore, and a person doesn't get that eerie feeling on walking past them; as if the restorations have chased all the ghosts away.

with the fiery little Jim Sloper, Jack kept peace and did much to brighten the camp. Reading, arguing with the others about politics or philosophy, and his constant rolling and smoking of cigarettes made the winter pass fairly pleasantly for him and gave him much time to think.

A Dangerous Woman

At the mouth of the Stewart River that winter lived many characters—Swedes, French Canadians, Germans, Irishmen, Texans, college graduates, illiterates, gamblers, showmen (Arizona Charley Meadows being the most prominent; he later built the Palace Grand Theatre in Dawson), men from all walks of life. Of all these, a wild American adventurer named Stevens made the deepest impression on Jack.

This man, who had the eyes of a merciless killer, might have been most dangerous person Jack London ever met, although Jack was probably too youthful and cocky to realize it at the time. Stevens also had the only woman in the entire area—and he meant to keep her.

Thoroughly macho in attire and gesture, Stevens had sought adventure as avidly as other men searched for gold, although he wanted that too.

In his 50 or so years he had gathered a spellbinding repertoire of stories in which rape, pillage and soldierly killing were the central theme. He could recount these adventures in such a vivid manner that no one who listened would doubt a word of it. The Nineteenth century was a period which spawned the idea of a "fearless Nordic conqueror" and Stevens considered himself a perfect embodiment of the breed. Only a certain type of woman could stay with such a man.

Stevens and this woman lived across the river. It so happened that the cabin of Jack London and his friends was the nearest and most prominent to the Stevens'. So, when the Stevens' crossed over the ice to visit the main camp, they would stop at the London cabin for an evening's talk.

The woman, under her heavy coat and fur hat, wore a rumpled, smoke-stained dress at least one size too small for her voluptuous figure. Her brown hair, oily from the lack of washing, hung in tangled locks. She brushed it away from her face with one hand in what, to the bachelors of Split-Up Island, was an exquisitely feminine gesture. Well into her prime, perhaps 30, she had held onto the timeless attributes of a woman who would be attracted to lusty, virile men.

Pouting lips always parted in an expectant breathlessness; dark, smouldering eyes that paused reflectively on the face of each man in the room; and a soft, husky voice which could break easily into a musical laughter—this was the only woman within hundreds of miles of frozen wilderness. With her coat off but hat still on, she sat in a chair beside Stevens or moved restlessly around the hot, crowded cabin, fully aware of the male eyes upon her.

On these memorable evenings the four occupants of the cabin had two sources of entertainment—Stevens' gory recitals or the sexy, posturing woman. In her case, she gazed unashamedly at young Jack London. Although she could not know, the ever-smiling Jack abhorred killing, even to feed himself.

She had come north, she said, on the advice of a strange spirit from another world who told her a man much older than she would lead her to fabulous riches. In spite of such a tale, every man in the cabin believed her to be highly intelligent. To Jack she was the most ideal vision of a "mate-woman" he had ever seen. And he wanted to see her again.

Three days after the Stevens' last visit Jack crossed the river to their cabin, in spite of the warnings of his mates. Again Stevens raved on with his stories until at last, winded, he stopped and the woman had a chance to talk to Jack.

Suddenly Stevens jumped up and, looking directly at Jack with shining, killer eyes, asked him if he would like to see some "straight shootin'." They went outside and the wildman put up a small metal target on a tree. He then fired ten shots into the target with such speed and accuracy that Jack was later to remark, *It was the quickest, straightest, surest shooting that I ever saw, and it gave me an uncanny, shivery feeling...that man...is afraid of nothing. Of nothing, I tell you..."*

Jack stayed away from the Stevens' after that. In later years he tried to find out what happened to them but no one seemed to know.

Sickness and Escape

When at last the ice broke up on the Yukon River, in May of 1898, Jack London had lapsed into a pitiful state. The five months of poor food and lack of exercise had brought the dread disease of the north—scurvy.

He had probably suffered from the lack of vitamins since the very beginning of his Yukon trip. His joints swelled up painfully and he had to walk bent over almost double. His remaining teeth loosened in their gums. His blistered skin became an inelastic, putty-like dough into which a dint poked by a finger would retain its shape for hours. Unsurprisingly, he was ready to quit the Klondike when the river cleared of ice and they were able to travel.

With a Doctor Harvey, who had come north to escape alcoholism, Jack made his escape. The two of them floated down the river toward Dawson on a raft built with logs from their cabin. Upon arriving there they sold the logs for six hundred dollars. Hordes of newcomers were arriving daily in the muddy town which was going through a spring flood. Jack went to see the famous Father Judge, the "Saint of Dawson," at his hospital and received medicine and curative vegetables for the scurvy.

On June 8, 1898, Jack and two other men headed downriver in a small, leaky, home-made boat. Their spirits were high, to say the least, even though they had 1500 miles of river ahead of them.

Meanwhile, Dawson was entering the peak year of the Gold Rush. Its population would reach 30,000 before summer's end. From every part of the world, over a network of trails and waterways, cheechakos frantically pushed toward the City of Gold. At the same time many parties like Jack's could be seen floating out of the country. The new arrivals paid no heed to the sorry tales of the outbound argonauts.

When Jack and his friends reached St. Michael on the Alaska coast, Jack was suffering a lot of pain. He was almost crippled from the waist down and couldn't straighten one leg. In spite of this, he had kept a descriptive diary of their trip, in which they had seen many Indian encampments and the earlier gold camps along the Yukon River.

But now it was time to get out of the country—or die.

A man called W.C. Prewitt felt so sorry for Jack that he gave him a ticket on the south-bound ship, the Bartlett. No other tickets being available, Jack's benefactor had to wait for another ship.

And so Jack London came home from the Klondike, arriving there one year after he had left for the Land of Gold.

Once more he decided to try writing for a living. At first his articles and stories didn't sell at all but he kept at it through another period of crushing poverty. Less than two years later his first book, *The Son of the Wolf*, was published. Jack went on from that to become the highest paid, best-known writer in the world. His work influenced later writers such as Hemingway, Steinbeck, Robert Service, Norman Mailer, Jack Kerouac and others—most of whom have never acknowledged his influence.

He continues to inspire fledgling writers today and he was the first creator of a romantic portrait of the Yukon.

Modern-day dancers at Diamond Tooth Gertie's Saloon in Dawson City.

A Christmas Carol
The Story of Edna Eldorado

Far from their homes in the south, three young prospectors mushed their team through the crackling cold. They had covered thirty miles that day over a narrow trail and had but three miles to go to reach their cabin on Eldorado Creek in the Klondike. It was Christmas Eve, 1897.

They suffered from the cold and, in spite of the time of year, wanted only to light a roaring fire to thaw their bones and relieve the searing pain in their chests. They paid no heed to the northern lights that had dropped a dancing curtain of ghostly colours over the frozen valley.

Then, in an open space to the right of the trail, they saw a lonely cabin almost enveloped in frost; the frost itself reflected the colours of the aurora borealis until cabin and sky were joined in a mystical scene, a scene that caused the young men to stop and stare. A faint wisp of smoke drifted from the stovepipe, as if to declare there was life within the cabin; but it was a life that was feeble and quiet.

"Let's go in and warm up," said Johnny Lind. They must have gone into Dawson for Christmas and we can get that fire going in no time."

They unlatched the door and tramped in. Dave Mitchell took a candle from his pocket and lit it in order to find the source of piteous moans coming from the bed in the corner. In the flickering candlelight he, Johnny Lind, and Bill Wilkinson beheld a sight they would remember for the rest of their lives.

A young woman lay on the bed with a newborn baby clutched to her breast. She stopped her faint cries to smile at Dave who quickly kneeled at her side. Her eyes, pain-filled yet satisfied somehow, opened wide for a moment, fluttered weakly, then closed in death.

The three young men stared at each other, stunned into silence, a silence the baby finally pierced with its shrill, life-filled cry.

While Johnny Lind built up the fire, Bill Wilkinson stripped off his many layers of clothing and even removed his new woollen underwear he had bought in Dawson that day. Quickly he wrapped the baby in the underwear and whatever blankets he could find. Just then the door burst open and another young man ran to the bedside.

"Jen! I've got the doctor!" He collapsed on the floor beside the bed and the doctor strode into the crowded cabin. He immediately checked the woman on the bed and the young man on the floor.

"Both dead. He froze his lungs with all the running he did today; it's forty-five below outside; and the mother... goddammit, these people should never have come north! Is there a woman around here you can take the baby to?"

"No," said Bill, who still held the baby in his huge arms. "Not close by there isn't."

"Well," said the doctor, "I've got

to be going. You'll have to take care of it somehow."

He packed his case and went out and the miners never saw him again.

They made a tiny bed from a packing box, tucked the baby into it, and dashed over the trail to their own cabin. Using a whiskey bottle and the finger from a leather glove, they fed the squalling child its first earthly meal: bear-stew broth with a tiny portion of brandy mixed in. The baby fell asleep in its box while the young men sang Christmas carols and gave thanks to whatever god they believed in.

But that isn't the end of the story.

Dave Mitchell set out the next morning to find a mother for their Christmas child. The news spread quickly and soon a dozen women arrived at the cabin; each were willing to adopt the baby, and the young miners faced a difficult decision. A Mrs. Brock stood back from the crowd, listening to the arguing, and finally she could stand it no longer.

"You're all a bunch of fools!" she exclaimed. "Give me that baby! You, Dave, take up a collection and get going into Dawson for some canned milk. Bring some clean blankets and some diapers too." She picked up the baby and held it with such a natural air that the boys knew the right decision had been made. Later they found out Mrs. Brock had lost a baby back in Nova Scotia; and here in the Klondike, by a miracle of events, she had found another.

For the rest of the winter the baby stayed in Mrs. Brock's cabin and it became the centre of attention on Eldorado Creek. The miners found a minister to baptize it in the spring and, after many suggestions, a name was chosen for the child; she was to be called Edna Eldorado. She was christened in an outdoor ceremony with gold nuggets and pokes of dust piled up around her. It was said that the toughest men in the north cried like babies on that spring day in the Klondike.

That is how the story has come down to us—through magazine and newspaper accounts and personal retelling—how three gaunt young prospectors were led by the northern lights to the side of a newborn babe on Christmas Eve in 1897.

Edna Eldorado cabin. Photo taken by noted geologist, J.B. Tyrell.

"My Heart Still Sings"

More dangerous than a raging tiger, more deadly than a desert rattler, more unstoppable than a charging bear—is a man of certain temperament.

Combine this temperament with a person who naturally hates women, usually because of a sour mother/son relationship, and we have a recipe for unfulfilled tragedy.

Along comes the bravest creature on earth—woman—spectacularly ill-equipped to handle danger—and the tragedy is played out, as it has been for thousands of years.

Mollie Walsh joined the Klondike Gold Rush in the fall of 1897. She came north in the company of a Presbyterian preacher who later said she was employed by an Irish linen manufacturer. An oldtimer from the American West said she had been a dance hall queen in Butte, Montana.

As smitten with the red-haired Mollie as any other man in Skagway, Reverend Dickey built the first church there. Mollie helped with fund raising and with the carpenter work itself. She became the darling of the town, singing hymns in the church and becoming a star member of the "Muffet and Crumpet Society."

When the Reverend decided to build a church at Bennett, on the other side of the famous mountain passes, Mollie moved too, setting up a restaurant at Log Cabin. A huge farewell party was held at Skagway to see her off. In his diary, the Reverend Dickey said, "Mollie never looked so lovely... There were tears on men's cheeks... Mollie sobbed openly and unashamed."

One of her first customers at Log Cabin was Jack Newman, packer, mule skinner, and all-around square shooter. Mollie helped him revive a frozen hand by rubbing his fingers—and Jack was smitten forever.

At the same time, though, Mollie was seeing a gambler who vowed to make Jack leave the country. Packer Jack heard about the gambler's boast and went down to Skagway for a duel. On Skagway's main street they went for their guns; Jack came out the winner after shooting his opponent in the leg. (He had promised Mollie he wouldn't kill the man.)

Mollie

Then Mollie, known as the "Angel of the Klondike Trail," got mixed up with another fellow by the name of Mike Bartlett, a pack train driver. Mike was loud, boisterous and said to be as mean as Packer Jack was gentle.

Jack came to Mollie's tent and confronted her, wanting her to make a choice. She did—she married Mike Bartlett and moved to Dawson City.

The couple left the Klondike with enough money to make a home in Seattle, Washington. Two and a half years later, in 1902, Mike Bartlett shot her dead on the street outside her home. She and Mike had separated and all she wanted was for him to leave her alone. Bartlett was acquitted of the murder charge by reason of insanity, the court calling it a "crime of passion," as they often did in those times. Later he committed suicide, leaving their son Leo an orphan.

Meanwhile, Packer Jack Newman had married but he never got over his love for the Irish maiden of his youth. In 1930, he had a statue made of Mollie and sent it

Jack

to Skagway. He didn't come for the ceremony but instead sent this telegram, which reads in part:

"...Her spirit fingers still reach across the years and play on the slackened strings of my old heart, and my heart still sings,—MOLLIE!—my heart still sings but in such sad undertone that none but God and I can hear."

PACKER JACK NEWMAN'S CABIN IN SKAGWAY, 1898

PACKER JACK NEWMAN'S TRAIN AT TOLLGATE, FIVE MILES FROM SKAGWAY, 1898

The Bishop Who Ate His Boots

The missionaries of the north get a lot of bad press these days. They are resented for their efforts to impose Christianity on natives and for their working with government to eradicate aboriginal culture. But in many cases it was only the missionaries who prevented native peoples from being destroyed by disease and mistreatment from the early settlers of the West and North.

Isaac Stringer, Bishop of the Yukon from 1905 to 1931, and his wife Sadie lived a life of fantastic adventure. Isaac came north first, to Herschel Island, where he made himself a great nuisance among the whaling fleets anchored there. Eventually he persuaded the captains of these ships to stop giving liquor to the Inuit people of the island.

His brought his wife to Herschel in 1896 where they lived four years in the back rooms of a warehouse full of walrus tusks and whalebone.

No longer able to get booze from the ships, an enterprising Inuit named Tonga built a still where he brewed a hellish mixture fermented from flour, molasses, raisins, yeast and—tobacco. Isaac haggled with the man over several months and finally bought the still from him and destroyed it. He and Sadie provided medical help to the natives and saved many lives during their stay. Two of the Stringer children, Rowena and Herschel, were born there and survived.

They worked their way south on a whaling ship. It took three months to reach San Francisco and when Sadie stepped off the gangplank she realized her clothes were totally out of fashion and she had no money for new ones. Soon they headed north again—Dawson City looked as good as Paris or London after their long stay at Herschel Island.

In 1909 Isaac and another man set out by canoe for Dawson from Fort McPherson. Winter came early and the rivers froze so they started walking. With only light clothing and few provisions, they found themselves facing an Arctic blizzard and soon were lost.

For three weeks they existed on supplies meant for three days. Each grew thinner and weaker and Isaac worried for his family. (Sadie was expecting another baby that month). He was determined to live to see them again. He remembered hearing an Indian legend about eating beaver skins. He and his partner had extra boots made of sealskin with whale-skin soles. They boiled the boots and toasted them over a fire.

They ate the top of the boots first, then the soles, and at last the middle. Both agreed that the sole was the best part.

With their strength almost gone, they came to a river and chopped a hole in it to see which way it flowed. It was the Peel River and following it downstream, they came at last to an Indian village. The peo ple of the village couldn't recognize the Bishop even after he called them by name.

A year later, on the same divide, four Mounties starved and died, one by one, after eating their dogs and leather sleigh traces. They were to be known forever as the Lost Patrol.

In another famous incident, told and retold by the oldtimers in the Klondike, Isaac got the final word in, as he usually did.

With his winter furs and rugged appearance, Isaac looked like many other denizens of the Far North. On this occasion he was driving his dogteam along a very rough trail when he met a trapper going the other way.

Isaac O. Stringer [Anglican Church photo]

"And how is the trail up ahead?" he asked the man.

The trapper roared, "It's a Goddamned son of a bitch. And what about the trail you've been over?"

Isaac answered, "Oh, about the same."

He was appointed Archbishop of Rupert's Land in 1931. He died in 1934, worn out from his epic travels. Sadie died in Vancouver in 1955.

CAPTAIN COURAGEOUS

* I sent this story to a national magazine. The lady editor replied, "Such things just don't happen."
Such things might not happen in a woman's world, or among the white collar set. But somewhere out in the ocean or perhaps on a little towboat on the MacKenzie River, a captain and crew are playing out the same kind of story I'm telling here.

I was twenty at the time—spring, 1968—and except for a few fights in school and a brief stint in the army, I had no experience of the rough life. I had never gone too long without food, never been attacked because of the colour of my skin, never been exposed to real danger. I enlisted in the Marines to fight in Vietnam. While I waited for them to call me up, I heard some fellows in a bar talking about the riverboats "way up north."

"No roads, man. Good money. See lots of country."

From Ottawa I travelled 3000 miles to Hay River, Northwest Territories. It was a town full of wildmen: trappers in with their furs, Icelanders from northern Saskatchewan getting ready to commercial fish on Great Slave Lake, construction crews, the boat crews, and lots of Indians. The streets were either muddy or dusty, depending on the weather. Wooden sidewalks with broken staves, built high in case another flood rolled in, lined the

At Hay River, N.W.T., May, 1968.

streets. At the time, Hay River had about 1000 permanent residents, but the population swelled to 3000 every spring.

I checked into the offices of the Northern Transportation Company.

"Hey, sonny, we have 2000 experienced deckhands to pick from. We're full up. Sorry."

I rented a shack in the Indian section of Old Town and went to the riverboat office every morning to ask for a job. In the meantime, I shovelled gravel, did other labouring jobs around town to survive. Forty-five mornings later the office manager said, "Get your ass down to the NT RICHARD first thing tomorrow. You'll be an apprentice deckhand this year unless someone quits or gets hurt; then we'll move you up. Captain George Moulton is the man to see."

By now I had fallen in love with a ballerina from Winnipeg. She had a summer job at The Hudson's Bay Store and I walked her home every night. She had to be in by nine o'clock, so, after I dropped her off that evening, I threw a little party in my shack. Just me and a couple of Indian girls.

Boom, bang, the door crashed open. In lurched seven half-drunk native youths, all about my age.

"White man, we're gonna cut your eyes out with this knife."

One of the girls heaved a bottle of beer and struck the biggest guy dead centre on the forehead. The other girl, I learned later, escaped through the back window.

The invaders broke the legs off an old wooden chair and using them as clubs, started pounding on me. Down I fell to the floor. Whack, crack went the chair legs on my head. I saw stars and tasted ozone on my tongue. I felt like fainting, but I had to keep my eyes on the knife poking at my face.

It all looked pretty hopeless.

Suddenly, silence. From my spot on the floor I turned sideways to see a canary-coloured stripe. The stripe ran right up the leg of the finest looking Mountie I ever saw.

"A young lady told us you were having trouble," he said. "Mr. Holloway, you'll have to help us identify your attackers. They cut out another fellow's eye down the street and he won't testify."

"Me neither," I said. "I have a boat to catch in the morning."

In the morning, the nurse in town taped my ribs, swathed my head with a long white bandage and gave me a pink patch for my eye. She wanted the doctor to stitch the back of my head and give me something for the pain.

"No time."

I limped down the dusty streets toward the docks and found my new home. I climbed over the rail of the NT RICHARD and threw my duffle bag on the deck.

"Who the hell are you?" came a shrill voice from the open wheelhouse window.

"I'm the apprentice deckhand."

"We don't take cripples on this boat. Go back downtown."

I stood there, silent. He turned away and I found another deckhand who showed me the crew's quarters. You had to open a hatch and look down a hole in the front of the boat. One side of the hole had a little steel ladder leading down. There were six bunks, three to a side, and there wasn't enough floor space for two men to dress at the same time. A steel bulkhead separated us from the engine room.

I climbed back on deck and met the mate: Walter—a Metis from Lake Winnipeg, as crabby-looking and worried as a man can get. He had a shriller voice than the captain.

"We're leaving this afternoon," he squeaked, "Gonna try and break through the ice on the Lake (Great Slave Lake, 300 miles long, 100 miles wide, said to be the deepest fresh water lake in the world).

The mate showed me my duties then fixed me up with a gallon of paint and a brush.

"Got to keep you fellows busy all a' time."

Then I met Donny, the only experienced deckhand on board. Long, black, uncombed hair with bits of fluff in it stuck out all round his hat. He looked grimmer than the mate and spoke with a whisky voice, hissing as he sucked in his breath through long, false teeth.

"With an effin mate like that, we're already in effin trouble," he growled and hissed. "Guy's from the effin Prairies. What the effin hell does he know? Nothin', that's what."

Lunch time. We clumped down to the galley, located below the main deck. The mate and Donny wore happy faces compared to the cook—old Cliff. He always looked as if he had just been stung on the ass by a bee and blaming you for it. The corners of Cliff's mouth dripped tobacco juice and he broke wind right there in the galley. His right hand was forever wiping tobacco juice off his face and then he cleaned his

The NT Richard

hand on his apron. The other fellows said all Cliff did besides cooking was drink Five-Star whisky—and sleep.

Old Cliff had a specialty, as all cooks do. The name of it is not fit to print. He scooped handfuls of dough from a pan and squashed them against his tobacco-stained apron. Then he flattened these pieces of dough with his fist on the counter. With one brown, tobacco-stained finger he folded them over and popped them in the oven. They were very tasty.

I'd have a run-in with the cook on our first trip out. Of course that was nothing compared to what was in store for me that season. It would be an adventure right up to the end, when old Skipper sank the boat.

In the meantime, on that afternoon of June 10, we lashed some 500-ton barges together with ropes as thick as your wrist, and headed out to the lake.

We never walked; we ran. We ran to grab cables, to lasso ballards, to pull 500-foot long, two-inch thick couplers out of the water, to take soundings, to bring Captain a coffee...it was run, run, run. No matter how fast we moved, old Skipper or Mate screamed at us all the time and called us terrible names.

The boat headed out to the wide expanse of the Lake. We hit the first patch of ice. The NT RICHARD tried to climb right up on top of it. Then we slid back down into the water and backed up and crashed into the ice again. And again.

We couldn't get through the ice. For three days we tried. The deckhands slept in the bow of the little ship, like I said before. Sleeping wasn't easy when the sides of your bedroom felt like they would

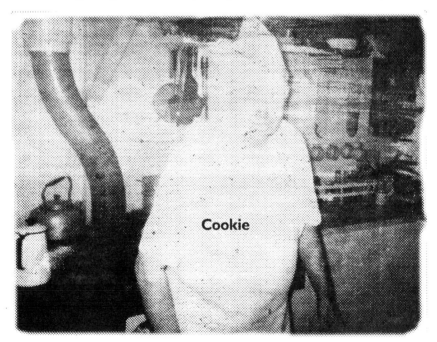

Cookie

buckle in at any moment. Between icebreaking and the roar of the big diesels, nobody slept much.

Captain George could scare the hell out of us with the power of that little boat. If he opened the engines to full power, the propellers (called wheels) could sweep all the water from under the boat till it literally sank to the bottom of the lake. But he always backed off just in time.

After a week of smashing around and returning to Hay River and heading back out again, we succeeded in crossing the Lake. At Wrigley Harbour, where the water of the Lake pours into the MacKenzie River, we dropped off the barges for another boat to pick up. It would take them downstream to points along the river or on Great Bear Lake.

I learned that the NT RICHARD was the only boat in the fleet that could handle the high waves and storms on the Lake. We would deliver all the orders for Yellowknife and the lodges and mining camps located around the lakeshore and then head down the MacKenzie for the Beaufort Sea.

We hit some savage storms. Waves crashed over the decks, old Cliff retired to bed, and we cooked for ourselves till the storm ended. During these times we had the chance to throw his gunny sack over the side. He used it to wipe the grill till it turned black and stunk like a dead raven. And he'd be furious to find it missing; said a new gunny sack made things stick to the stove.

Rocking and reeling, engines roaring, the little RICHARD stopped for nothing. Someone, usually me, had to man the towline at the stern of the boat, ensuring it didn't get so slack it dragged bottom, or tight enough to break. I had to lash myself to the winch so as not to be carried overboard by the waves.

Great Slave Lake.
We are about to smash our way through the ice enroute to the MacKenzie River.

To ride out a storm in a small towboat can make you sick or give you a feeling of being utterly alive. The sensations of motion and sound, the twisting and turning, the rattle of equipment, the sudden roar of the engines when the props left the water after cresting a high wave...there was no time for fear, no time to think at all, and who could think with all that racket?

Cookie's pots and pans clashed together on their hooks in the galley; dishes slid back and forth on the table. Ropes, chains, barrels, everything not welded down slid back and forth like a noisy pendulums. Some members of the crew got seasick. Old Skipper, one of the engineers—Oliver, I think, and myself liked to sing hymns in the wheelhouse during storms. On calmer days we recited Robert Service in unison.

One day we lost a barge in a storm. We found it where the Slave River enters the Lake. We tied a cable round some trees to anchor the boat as the wind got stronger and stronger. The wind howled over the water, and, believe it or not, swept it away in the shallower spots. We could see fish floundering on the mud, gasping with their gills for water that wasn't there. The wind picked up some of the mud from the bottom and flung it at the boat and we were days cleaning it off.

Then the Lake would calm down suddenly, the waves would slowly even out and flatten, and it was if we floated on a sea of glass.

The worst was offloading cargo at the various villages around the Lake. Not because of the work, although we often worked forty hours straight, but because of the mosquitoes and black flies.

Besides a crabby mate, we had an ever-complaining purser. His job was to check off the crates as we offloaded them. We lost our purser because of the mosquitoes.

He literally went insane. He swung his clipboard wildly to clear the air of mosquitoes but the moment he tried to write they were at him again, covering his face and hands.

One afternoon the purser disappeared off the deck. We searched everywhere.

"He's gone to the bush, jumped ship," said Captain.

Then someone tried to take a shower and there was the purser hiding there with the water pouring over him.

He wouldn't come out of his mosquito-free haven. We had to drag him out and send for a plane to take him back to Hay River.

We delivered the annual food supply to an Indian village called Rat River. Some of the locals came down to the boat to look around and sit in the galley. I noticed the mosquitoes didn't bother these people.

I soon learned their secret: woodsmoke, raw furs, and no washing since time began—that was their recipe for keeping mosquitoes at bay.

I didn't tell you why the cook got mad at me.

It was the apprentice deckhand's job to wash the decks every day. I did this by throwing a pail over the side and pulling it up with a rope. After soaping the deck, I'd heave pails of water across it to rinse it off.

Old Cliff baked bread and his special buns every morning. After they came out of the oven, he'd set them on the table to cool, then open the hatch above the table...

I let go with a pail of water...just as Cookie opened his hatch...you know the rest. I had to stay out of the galley for a week and have someone bring me my meals.

And the mate too had it in for me. I had painted the ladder going up to his quarters with nice black paint but forgot to tell him. When he reached the top of the ladder and saw his blackened hands, he went into a terrible rage. He still thinks I did it on purpose. The rest of the crew thought so too.

One day I slipped on the wet steel deck and fell between two 1000-ton barges. Just as they were about to smash together, Donny pulled me up out of there with a rope. Then I saved his life a few days later. As he leaped from one barge to another his foot slipped and he didn't make it all the way across. I caught his hand and pulled him up somehow.

In those days the smaller settlements in the Arctic didn't have fuel storage tanks. Every bit of gas and diesel fuel came in drums. We would roll thousands of fuel drums down wooden ramps onto the shore and then stand them up. From all over the village, children came rolling the empties from the previous year. Then we'd stack the empties on the barge, tie them down and take them back to Hay River.

We hauled fuel in tanker barges across the Lake to Yellowknife. This was an easy job compared to freight. As the fuel was being pumped off we could go uptown and drink in the bars. We couldn't chase women; the few single women had so many guys

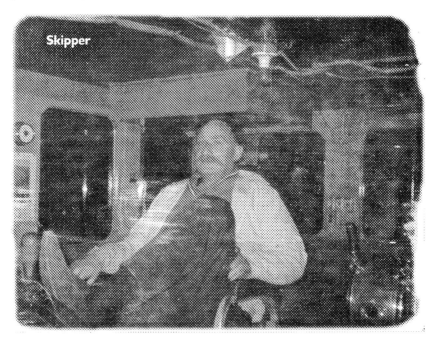

Skipper

chasing them that they wouldn't look twice at a lowly deckhand from a barge company.

One of us always had to watch the boat while the rest went uptown. One night it was my turn. A young fellow came alongside the dock, said he'd like to look over the boat.

I showed him around, gave him coffee and some of Cookie's buns, and he left.

Next morning, Skipper noticed his binoculars and transistor radio gone from the wheelhouse.

Did I catch hell. But the thief returned a couple of weeks later.

I was watching the boat again. Late evening. A visitor, the same guy, half-drunk this time. I tried to radio the Mounties and keep this fellow on board, but couldn't get through.

So I wrestled him down and tried to tie him up with some small rope. He got away and jumped down onto the deck. He fell on his side and broke a wine bottle that was in his pocket. It cut his forearm wide open. He bled all over the dock. I thought he would bleed to death, the damn thief, so I got him back on board, blood all over the place, and wrapped a towel round his arm.

I said, "We'll have to wait for someone to come along; I'm not letting you go."

He said, "Do something for this cut."

I heated water in a large basin, poured in a can of Gillett's Lye, a bottle of iodine, and some turpentine, added some salt and pepper.

"Stick your arm in there," I told him.

Which he did. The bleeding stopped immediately. He jumped up and ran out onto the deck and from there leaped down onto the dock. Around and around he went, doing an Indian war dance, whooping and crying at the night sky.

Just then Captain and the crew arrived in a taxi. They saw my "prisoner" prancing around on the dock, holding his arm in the air.

"Get him," I hollered. "That's the son-of-a-bitch stole Skipper's binoculars."

We held him till the Mounties came and they took him away. I heard they let him go because nobody could prove anything anyhow.

After that the fellows on the boat called me, "Doc."

We finished up on Great Slave Lake and started loading cargo for a trip down the Mackenzie River. The Mackenzie is 1100 miles long and has the largest drainage basin of any river in Canada, the total length of the system being 2600 miles. Only the St. Lawrence River pours more water into the ocean. It is fed mainly by Great Slave Lake which in turn is filled by the Peace and Athabasca rivers along with countless smaller streams. Part way down the Mackenzie, the rapid-filled Liard River joins in. Many smaller rivers join up farther on.

We'd be going all the way to Colville River, on the north shore of Alaska. An oil company had started drilling there and we would take in the drills, drilling muck, Nodwells, and stuff like that. Later on this area would be known as the Alaska's North Slope.

A pilot came on board to guide us as far as Arctic Red River. He was an Indian from Hay River by the name of Gabe. Gabe worried about nothing, always had a funny story to tell, and knew the river like some people know their aches and pains. He was the only calm human being I was to encounter for the next several months and I stayed by to listen to him as much as I could. He knew stories about the Headless Valley, and told me Indian legends about every landmark or mountain along the way.

Our cranky mate had quit or got fired, and Donny was long gone. The new mate, Carl Berg, was a pleasure to work with. He knew, we knew he knew, and so everyone listened well. I'm sorry to say Carl and I parted on bad terms, but that wouldn't happen for a long time yet.

At Fort Simpson we unloaded a bit of freight and picked up a new deckhand to replace Donny.

He has to be dead by now, he was half-dead then, but I never met a man like old Bud.

He drank, he swore, he was so stiff he shuffled his feet to walk, and could do anything at all. He could run any kind of machinery, tie any kind of knot, figure out any kind of towing arrangement...he always knew just what to do. If I've forgotten all the tricks he taught me, I never forgot the style he had.

I didn't know it at the time, but old Bud and Captain liked me a lot. I was young, tried so hard, and made so many mistakes. They yelled at me and called me names and ignored me when I tried to talk to them. When old Bud left us at Aklavik, he gave me a pair of boots and some gloves.

"Old Bud never gives anything away; remember that, Sam." said Skipper.

Halfway down the MacKenzie, just before Fort Good Hope, are some limestone cliffs called the Ramparts. There we ran into trouble.

The barges had to be relayed through this narrow gap in the river, one at a time. On one of these relays, we punched a hole in the boat.

The engineer grabbed a side of Cookie's bacon and stuffed it in the hole.

"We've got to tie up the boat!"

The Ramparts

screamed the Captain, "So they can fix the goddammed leak!"

He blamed the trouble on the Bennett Dam in British Columbia. They had closed the gates that summer and all the rivers in the north were suffering low water.

Anyhow, it was black night and raining. The high cliffs loomed on both sides of us. A young deckhand named Tim had bragged all season about his mountain-climbing escapades in the Canadian Rockies.

"Tim, you climb up there with a rope. Sam will go with you," said Skipper. "I'll shine the arc lights on you and tell you how you're doing through the megaphone."

We started up the cliff, Tim leading, showing me the hand holds. It was hard to see with the shadow created by the bright lights on our backs. We made it up about thirty feet. I heard Tim scream and he hurtled past me into the void below us.

And Captain yelled through the megaphone, "Did you think you were Jesus Christ? Even he couldn't walk on air, you stupid bastard!!"

Tim lay silent far below me. I could see his outline in the sand as Captain lowered the lights.

Anyone who has climbed mountains knows that going down is more dangerous than going up. You can't see where to place your feet and you have to look down all the time. The temptation to jump is sometimes hard to push out of your head.

I elected to go up. I went another twenty feet and heard a noise just below me. It was Tim. To his everlasting credit, after he had regained the wind that had been knocked out of him from his fall, he started climbing again. Once at the

top of the cliff, we used the rope to haul a cable up and tied up the boat. Coming down was easy, using the rope again.

The engineers welded the hole and on we went toward the Beaufort Sea and many more adventures.

Half the ducks and geese in North America nest along the lower reaches of the Mackenzie River during summer. The noise and wash from the boat sent them skyward till they darkened the day around us. Bears and wolves stared curiously at us from the riverbanks.

Captain liked to take pot shots at animals along the shore, using a scope-mounted .22 rifle. He hit a bear once and it squealed, sounding like a woman in terrible pain, and ran along the shore and then off into the woods. Later on Skipper would shoot at seals.

A kind of rage was building within me as the days wore on. Except for the trips to Yellowknife, we worked seven days a week, for all of our waking hours.

The Mackenzie is not a deep river. Our boat had a draft of five and a half feet, too much for river work, and we always had to know the depth ahead. Someone, often me, had to stand on the lead barge with a sounding pole, dipping it and telling Skipper over a walkie-talkie the number of feet of water. Sometimes my pole would stick in the mud and I'd lose it. Rather than face Captain's rage, I'd hurry back to the boat for another pole, telling him phony depth readings, praying we didn't hit a sandbar or rock.

At Aklavik, our last stop before heading out into the delta-lands, we picked up three cat-skinners (bulldozer operators). They were from Texas. Big they were, and full of confidence.

Within a few days they'd all wish to die.

Like I already mentioned, the NT RICHARD was built as a lake boat. We weren't supposed to be travelling rivers and opinion held that no one but Captain George could get us through the MacKenzie Delta. Then we'd face the Arctic Ocean. We weren't supposed to go there with this boat, either.

We went up one channel and down another, trying this one and that. Sometimes we got stuck. The crew took out the lifeboat and threw off a heavy anchor, then Captain would winch us off the bottom so we could go up some other channel.

One day we broke out into the ocean. Giant whales spouted in the distance. The boat took on a new type of ride on the ocean swells. Seals followed us in coveys, waiting for Cookie to throw more slops over the side. Seagulls perched on the afterdeck and my job was to clean up after them.

All during the season, every hour or so, a deckhand had to fetch Skipper or Mate a coffee, carrying it from the galley, up one deck, then up a ladder to the wheelhouse. During rough weather it was quite a job.

One of our crew, we who took all the abuse, thought of a way to get this coffee delivered: He filled two cups full of coffee and set them in a pot with a handle on top. Then he carried the pot to the wheelhouse window, dumped one cup of coffee into the other and handed Skipper a brimful cup through the open window.

One day Skipper asked him, "How come you're the only son of a bitch on this boat that brings me a full cup of coffee?"

"That's easy," said the deckhand. "When I'm in the galley,

The NT Husky

I take a great big mouthful; when I get up here, I spit it back in the cup."

George spit out the coffee and threw the cup over the side. The deckhand was about to be thrown off the boat, in the middle of the Arctic. But he confessed his method instead.

Old Oliver, the engineer, had sailed all his life. If you opened a can upside down and set it on the galley table, Oliver would grab it and heave it over the side.

"Bad luck on a ship to open a can upside down," he'd say. He had lots of other superstitions, all gained from bigger ships than the RICHARD.

One day the mate sent me up to paint the inside of the engine flumes. These are large, high air scoops that funnel air down to the engine room.

I started painting. I looked down to see Oliver walking about in the engine room far below. I yelled, "Oliver!"

My voice echoed down the pipes. I saw Oliver lift his ear protectors from his head and look all around, everywhere but up. I yelled again; it sounded like a banshee from the Scottish moors. He lifted the ear muffs again; stared all around.

For the next two days I would yell down the flume, periodically. At mealtimes, Oliver would sit at the galley table, across from me, not saying a word.

I often wondered who he thought was calling him.

We started out across the Beaufort Sea, heading for Herschel Island. The ocean swells grew larger and larger.

Up in the wheelhouse the three big Texans entertained Skipper with tales of adventure. The wheelhouse, being the highest spot on the boat, rocked back and forth with ever greater motions.

The biggest Texan was the first to head for the rail. All we could see were his broad hips as he called for *"Geooorge! Geooorge! Billlll! Billllll!"* and the puke hung down in strings from his face.

His buddies laughed. The waves got higher. One after another, they too headed for the rail.

Skipper laughed till the tears rolled down his face. His eyes squinted shut till he couldn't see where we were going. He'd stop laughing till he looked over toward the rail at the three Texans then he'd start again. He began to sing one of his favourite hymns; it was the only way he could control himself. The Texans made it down to the galley and vomited all over it. Finally we had to help them to their bunks (in the crew's quarters) and tie them in so they wouldn't fall to the floor.

One of them begged for a gun so he could shoot himself. Perhaps physical size has something to do with how seasick one can get. Being small, I was like the Captain— the rougher it got the better I liked it. It made you feel so alive—connected to Mother Earth in all her violence and beauty—ready to yank you back to her womb at any moment...

A heavy fog, so thick it wet your hands and face, surrounded the boat . Skipper, using radar and maps, steered us to Herschel Island. At Pauline Cove, we buried a dead man (a log in the sand) and tied up the boat. We sat for ten days waiting for the fog to lift. In the meantime we deckhands explored the island and the old ghost town left from the whaling days.

The fog lifted and we towed the barges to the coast of Alaska. Just as we were anchoring them individually, a great storm blew up. Twenty-foot waves crashed all around us. The water sprayed onto the steel decks and formed ice as smooth as glass. At that time of year in the far north, the days are short. We worked in darkness a lot, using miner's headlamps. If one of had fallen overboard, no one would miss him for hours. It was every man for himself. If you couldn't be picked up by the boat, you stayed out on the barge till the weather calmed down.

The next two hours were the most dangerous of all our lives, I think. We had turned the barges loose so we could anchor them one at a time. Now they were scatter-ing all over the Beaufort Sea. Captain would get as close to one as he could and a deckhand had to leap across, timing his jump carefully. As one vessel went up on a wave, the other was coming down till there was forty feet difference in their heights. We all did it, jumping across as the barges were level for a split-second, landing on ice and skidding halfway to the other side. Once on a barge we let out an anchor to hold it there. Then Skipper would streak by and we'd try and get aboard. Once, he got too close and the barge and boat smashed together with a horrendous buckling of steel.

All the while, the Mate and Skipper screamed and hollered at us and we couldn't hear what they said because of the storm and then they'd really get mad and call us all sorts of names.

Without serious mishap, we an-

The towline, with the first barge just in sight. In the Beaufort Sea enroute to Colville River, Alaska.

chored the damn barges. Suddenly the sea calmed down, the waves smoothed out gradually, and an American boat came to pick up the barges and the three Texans, who were still abed.

On the way back to the Delta, we hit another storm. An anchor came loose on the afterdeck and was smashing around, destroying everything in its path. Tim, the mountain climber, tried to tie it down and it caught him across the legs.

For three days he lay in his bunk with broken legs. We had nothing to give him but aspirin. Finally the weather cleared enough for a float plane to land and take him to the hospital in Inuvik.

At Inuvik a few days later we picked up some empty barges and headed upstream on the MacKenzie. It took three times as long as coming down from Hay River, about twenty-one days pushing against the current. Except for relaying barges through fast parts of the river, the deckhands had it easy for the first time in three months.

At last we arrived at Hay River and within the hour were sent back out with full barges. The Company pushed the Captains to deliver as much cargo as possible before freezeup; they in turn had to push the boats and, of course, the crews. We hauled more stuff to Yellowknife, Snowdrift and other settlements. By now it was October, approaching Thanksgiving. About two weeks to go before the boat would be drydocked for the season. Besides the Captain, I was the only one left who had started out the season on the NT RICHARD.

We went up the Slave River to Bell Rock, near Fort Smith. There we took on a load of lumber from a sawmill.

And I jumped ship.

At the time I was among the bitchiest, snarliest, most contrary group of men ever to congregate in such small quarters as the NT RICHARD. Not a man had anything nice to say about anyone else. Cookie (the third since the season began) complained from morning to night. The engineers stopped speaking to each other and even Skipper and Mate were at odds over something. We were all beat, wanted to get to hell back to Hay River then home.

I broke a tie-rod end on a big fork lift I was driving. The mate proceeded to dress me down. I showed him the tie-rod end, already broken three-quarters through. He continued to scream how stupid I was.

The injustice was too much for my system at the time. I packed my duffle bag and threw it on the dock. Captain continued the tirade.

"We'll have you in jail by morning! You goddamm ship-jumper!" And on and on.

A fuel truck had driven out from Fort Smith to fuel up the boat. I asked the driver for a ride into town.

The captain yelled through his megaphone: "Don't you give that son of a bitch a ride! Make him walk!"

The truck's taillights vanished down the road. I turned round and ran for the dock, flying through the air and landing on the deck of the RICHARD. In a flash I was in the wheelhouse and reached for Captain's throat to throttle him.

The mate, twice my size and a lot tougher, grabbed me from behind. He and the another deckhand threw me off the boat. I landed hard but was unhurt. I stood there and watched the boat disappear into the mists of the river.

Black, black was the night. I started down the trail to Fort Smith and walked along it, slowly, sometimes stopping to feel with my hands for the road. I heard a great thumping in the bush to my right and then a strange, loud bellow.

Buffalo. I was near Woods Buffalo Park.

My kit-bag weighed a hundred pounds. I threw out all my extra boots and clothes and kept walking. I heard a new sound then and saw a pair of headlights.

It was the fuel truck driver, coming back to pick me up. He restored my faith in the human race. If you read this, my friend, here is a belated thank you.

At the hotel in Fort Smith I met two drunken truck drivers. Once the bar closed, we climbed into their Kenworth and drove down the gravel road toward Hay River. I thought they were driving the old truck pretty fast for the gear they were in.

Suddenly the engine flaps flew up, flames shot out on both sides of the hood, and the truck stopped. With only room for them to sleep, they kicked me out and I walked down the road in the dark, with a hundred and fifty miles to go. It was cold enough to freeze the water in the pot holes.

Dawn came. A car approached me and stopped. I read the sign on the side, NORTHERN TRANSPOR-TATION COMPANY. The driver rolled down his window.

"We'll be back from Smith tomorrow. Pick you up then. Right now we're in a hurry. *ONE OF OUR BOATS SANK LAST NIGHT.*"

I blurted, "The RICHARD?"

They looked surprised but didn't ask how I knew.

I caught a ride later that day and checked into the company offices at Hay River. I asked them if anyone was killed on the RICHARD.

"No, but the boat's a write-off.

"Lucky I wasn't there 'cause I can't swim," I said.

"Who are you?"

I told them my name. My name was mud.

"You're the son of a bitch jumped ship on George! He was so mad he sank the boat!"

"Can you give me an advance on my pay?" I asked.

"Hey, you won't need an advance. You're being charged. Jumping ship is a criminal offense. We'll nail you with assault, too."

I walked out. I had exactly 35 cents in my pocket. All my pay cheques had been sent to a bank in Ottawa. It was Friday, Thanksgiving weekend; nothing open till Monday.

I hid in an old cabin outside Hay River that night. In the morning I stood by the road, ready to run if a police car came in sight. A big Meteor sedan pulled up and stopped.

"I'm heading for Edmonton," said the driver. "You can ride along but don't ask for money or anything to eat."

We drove for three days. The driver, a cook from one of the boats, told me about his apartment building in Edmonton and how he bought a new Meteor every three years. He stopped at restaurants and stayed at a motel two nights. I sat in the car all the while, nursing a quart of milk I had bought with my 35 cents.

At last, Edmonton. I tried to get some money from a bank. Not enough identification, they said. Sorry.

I slept in a ditch outside Edmonton that night, covering myself with the clothes I hadn't thrown away. In the morning, with a light snow falling, I hitchhiked to Calgary. By now I hadn't eaten for almost five days. The banks there wouldn't talk to me either. In Ottawa I had almost five thousand dollars in the bank, a lot of money in 1968.

A miracle. On a sidestreet in Calgary, I ran into Tim, the deckhand who had broken his legs. He still limped a bit but had pretty well recovered. He took me to his father's house for something to eat. Tim's dad took me down to his bank and they let me have a thousand dollars of my money.

I flew home to Ottawa. My mother said that for months I talked in my sleep about barges and ballards and anchors and such. And I swore a lot more than before I left.

EPILOGUE

I bought an almost-new Chevy with my earnings, forgot about going to Vietnam, and found myself a girlfriend in Ottawa.

The following year, 1969, the boat company sent me a letter asking me to come back and work for them. I declined, being engaged for marriage and working as an apprentice electrician. Besides, my ego

hadn't fully recovered from the last voyage, though I appreciated that I had had a grand adventure.

It wasn't long till I headed north again. In 1982, I was operating a small power station on Southhampton Island. That's a big island in the middle of Hudson's Bay in the eastern Arctic. The annual supply ship pulled into harbour. It was a real ocean-going vessel, very impressive. Down the ramp walked a vaguely familiar figure.

It was Captain George, my old skipper on the NT RICHARD.

We talked, ate dinner on the ship, parted as friends. I know now that it takes tough men for tough jobs. A nice-mannered, gentle person who might treat you ever-so-humbly probably couldn't be a ship's captain, spending year after year in the company of roughnecks and storms. In the movies you can be a fist-fighting demon, shoot everyone in sight, and then be a gentleman down at the schoolmarm's house. Not so in real life.

So, here's to you Captain George, and to all men like you, wherever you may be.

The author on the afterdeck of the NT Richard, 1968.

The Ghosts of Dawson

In the winter of 1986, I holed up in Dawson City and I had the saddest neighbour you could imagine. He was an old Malemute husky and he sat on his doghouse roof all winter "howling out his woes to the homeless snows" until I thought I would lose my mind.

Whenever he ceased his plaintive discourse, another husky at the lower end of town would take up the refrain. The only times my neighbour's melancholy would brighten were when I threw him a piece of steak or moose liver. While the dog munched happily, a raven—the same raven all the time—would sit on top of a frosted power pole, cackling hideously as he waited for a chance to steal the meat from the husky.

Sometimes it became unbearable (I was trying to write the great Yukon novel at the time) and I would take a stroll downtown. Dawson City in December is not a lively place. Especially when it's 40 below and the Dome mountain casts its three-month shadow over the town. I'd have a coffee at the Downtown, another at the Eldorado, and visit my friend Chum at Chum's Crafts or else have tea with Father Bob. Then, in the darkness, wrapped in my long Arctic parka and shuming my snow packs along the frozen streets, I'd walk by the haunted places of the city that was built on the lust for gold.

Jack London (or somebody with a John Kennedy hairdo and a white shirt) would wave from the open window frame of his cabin; I would see him ever so clearly even though they put him in the darkest corner they could find at the bottom of the Dome. Just across from Roy McDiarmod's garage, an old weather-blackened shop leaned over precariously as if it were about to spew itself onto the street. In the bay windows on the second floor an old woman sat; she knitted as she rocked back and forth in her chair and she always looked wistfully towards uptown as though she watched for a wayward man to come home from the saloon.

After that I would walk along Front Street by the river, where the Stampeders built their gambling halls and thousands of men and women used to promenade from one establishment to another. Perhaps it was just the Yukon River murmuring under its prison of ice, but I often heard a multitude of voices—subdued voices—as I walked alone along the quiet street. One night I stopped in front of where the old Monte Carlo Palace of Pleasure once stood. My mind, perhaps my whole being, drifted back through time to December, 1898. Here's what I saw:

The sky was the limit on the gaming tables and sulky, painted sirens watched with greedy yet lively eyes while the men from the creeks displayed and tossed around their wealth. Klondike Kate cavorted on the stage trailing 50 yards of chiffon behind her, balancing a brace of lighted candles on her head. Cad Wilson rasped out drippy songs of heartbreak, romance, and home while the Klondike Kings sent gleaming gold nuggets clattering onto the stage.

The entertainers stepped down and men's voices blended into a dull roar and punctuated by the yells of a lucky gambler or the shrieks of a half-drunk whore. Then, into the smoke and alcohol fumes, strutted the Kid.

He may have been the Burn-Em-Up Kid, the Chills-And-Fever Kid, the Evaporated Kid, the Granulated Kid. the Hot-Cake Kid, the Jagtime Kid, the Nanny-Goat Kid, the No-Shirt Kid, the Yellow Kid, the Ping Pong Kid, the Sealskin Kid, the Skylight Kid, the Wake-Up Kid, the Down-And-Out Kid, or the Gold Dust Kid. Into the corner he darted, gesturing to another man at the blackjack table. The two of them slipped out the door. Another pair of men followed, then groups of three, four, five, left until the hall had only a few well-dressed men at the bar. And, of course, the ladies.

"Another big strike somewhere; probably a bust," said Diamond Lil Davenport. "They'll be back soon, with a sack of gold or a broken heart. We'll fix them up either way, won't we girls?"

She looked around at her friends. Mollie Fewclothes, Ethel the Moose, Touch-The-Button Nell, Clawfinger Kate, the Grizzly Bear (she was six feet tall and had only one eye), Nellie the Pig, Ping Pong, Gumboot Sue, Glycerine and Vaseline—all of these stout ladies (don't forget; they had to climb the Chilkoot Pass to get into the Yukon) were as tough and determined to get some gold as any of the miners digging in the frozen ground. And probably a lot smarter.

Swiftwater Bill, Nigger Jim Dougherty, and Big Alex MacDonald stood talking at the bar—they already had enough gold. To one side Jack London slouched, his feverish, scurvy-yellow eyes glowing as he soaked up treasures of another sort: tales of hardship and bravery and fabulous fortunes. Outside the saloon, Father Judge, the Saint of Dawson, trudged past pulling a sleigh with another patient for his hospital lashed onto it: another Klondiker had succumbed to the cold and the lack of food.

Ah yes, I saw a lot on my winter strolls through the streets of Dawson City. Spend a winter there sometime; you'll like it.

Spring in Dawson, 1985

With Friends Like These...

Folks in Dawson City tend to look down their noses at local "characters." I guess it has always been so, but they forget that a group of characters built the City of Gold in the first place. Upright folks took over from the miners and sporting women and made the original inhabitants feel very unwelcome.

I say this because I felt the effects of that disdain when I lived there. Not because of who I was (not much of I anything) but who I chose as friends.

Windy Farr lived in a house near the Moosehide Slide. He could recite the name and captain of every boat that sailed the Yukon River. He collected bent nails, magazines, driftwood, and other odds and ends. Most of this he kept in his house to the extent that he had no room for a bed. He slept in a chair near the door.

When Windy told a story in that wonderful clear voice of his, he could | make the world recede better than any movie or popular song. I thought he was the most wonderful human being I met in the Klondike.

Fightin' Bob Russell, born at Fortymile and raised in the bush, took me on some of the most harrowing prospecting trips that any cheechako could possibly imagine. One time a grizzly bear rushed right past us in a swamp, going the opposite way. I figured that bear knew old Bob was moving in and it was time to clear out. We actually found a lost gold mine (another column) after walking many miles through a huge swamp. Anybody but Bob would have gotten lost for sure.

But in town, Bob just never fit

The late Windy Farr, with a welcoming smile at his home in Dawson.

in. I believe he is the finest bushman to ever walk the north and the most authentic citizen of Dawson City.

Anton (Tony) Fritz. Opportunist extrordinaire. Always had a new scheme, right up till he died at the age of 81.

Tony had a huge old Ford sedan that he licensed as a taxi. It was so big he practically disappeared in it but it kept him in gambling money for Gerties. One time a woman called from the Downtown Hotel. She was very drunk at the time. Tony pulled up to fetch her and she staggered down the steps onto the long white veranda, which had just been painted. She ran smack into one of the white columns and wrapped herself around it and slid to the deck.

She raised herself and stumbled toward the taxi, where Tony stood with h back to her, talking to someone. H turned around and watched with horror' as the painted lady lost her balance an fell against his beloved Ford.

She slid to the ground but reached up for a door handle and opened it. Tony sprang into action, grabbing her hair and clothes until the two of them fell down. By the time the fight was over and the Mounties came, the cab, Tony, and the lady were equally decorated with white paint and mud.

The Dawsonites who saw it though it was a disgusting scene. I thought it was the funniest show of all time.

Captain Dick Stevenson lived in an old rusty school bus near Tony's place Oh, the stories we swapped in that old bus. Dick invented the world famous Sourtoe Cocktail,

Captain Dick watching a young lady drink a sourtoe cocktail. He has his spare toe between his teeth.

which was merely a pickled human toe dropped into a drink. (You can see that toe between Dick's teeth in the photograph.)

Dick had an old Ford truck he used to haul firewood. The steering box went on it and he replaced it with one from an old Dodge. Now, when you turned the steering wheel left, the truck would go right, and vice versa. Dick would bring wood from across the river and back that truck onto the ferry. One time he bet a young fellow ten bucks that he couldn't drive it around the block. The boy wound up in an old basement with the truck and Dick almost died laughing.

He melted some brass into some pretty fair looking gold (brass) nuggets. At Diamond Tooth Gertie's, he had the habit of throwing one nugget at a time behind the curtain as the dancing girls finished their show. You could hear them fighting and scrambling back there over that nugget. Finally they realized the trick and complained to the KVA about Dick. But like the man says, you can't sucker anyone who isn't greedy.

Captain Dick and I both peddled books in Dawson City. In a bar crowded with tourists, he would shout, "Sam, do you have any of those best-selling books of yours?"

"Yes, I do! And do have any of those famous books of yours, or are they all gone?"

I recall him autographing a book for a rather stout, rather matronly lady tourist. I saw her gazing at the autograph with a strange look on her face so I went over to see. He had inscribed it so:

"To the lady I'd most like to f___k! Yours truly, Captain Dick."

How could he not be respected in Dawson City after pulling a class act like that?

The late Bob Russell and his daughter. That's Prospector Jim White in the boat. We were about to take off on a bar mining trip down the Stewart River.

Baking by the Sack

The photo below was taken on one of the creeks around Dawson in 1898—a hundred years ago.. The black woman is a "Lady of the Evening," perhaps twenty-five years old. The signs for 'cigars' and 'baking by the sack' told the miners what she really specialized in. The miner, who appears to be in his late forties, smoking his pipe, has brought her a gift and the empty box lies on the ground. What do you suppose was in the box? Who laid the cobblestones in front of her cabin door? What were the titles of the books in the window? Did she have a good education? Was he one of the original goldminers on the rich creeks?

A broken, hand-operated washing machine lies on its side to the right of the cabin. Most of the trees on the hillside behind have been cut down. The cabin itself was built in a hurry, with some of the logs unpeeled. Did she own the cabin or was she renting it?

The sun is just setting behind

the cabin so it is probably about ten o'clock on a summer evening. The couple seem to be good friends. She is holding her cat on her shoulder. He has his boots all laced up tightly, so he has probably just arrived and is hoping to spend the night.

She might have stayed in the Klondike a few years before leaving for the south, and she probably had a pretty good stake to set up her new life. The miner is likely buried somewhere in the Yukon. In any case, they have been in their graves for many years, their time on earth forgotten by the world except for this chance photograph. I found this picture in a box at Jim Robb's house one evening in the winter of 1986.

So here we have two ordinary people in their moment of eternity, making the best of what they had, before (as we all must) descending into the dust of time.

Gold Specks and Ulcers

Sometimes an event, a person, or even a book, can change the entire course of our lives. In my case, an old Yukon hermit gave my life a twist and I don't know whether to thank him or curse him.

At the time I was trying hard to be what my family, wife, and society thought I should be: a steady Eddy. I had a career with the power company and they had sent me to Mayo, Yukon, to work on the old hydro plant there.

Just below the dam lived a spotted dog and his wretched old master—in a cave the old man had dug for himself into the high, sandy bank of the Mayo River. Folks said around Mayo that the hermit brought gold into town on a regular basis from his claim there on the riverbank. Over the years he wrote a book and one day went south to get it published, and to bring back some mining equipment.

In the Yukon he fit right in, being no more self-centred or strange than any of us, but in Vancouver they locked him away in an asylum. He never returned to his claim and cave.

I staked his gold claim when it lapsed. My job was giving me ulcers and I wanted something to do on weekends. One afternoon I went there with a pan to try my luck.

In the very first pan, three rice-sized nuggets of gold shone up at me. A chill raced up and down my spine. I remember gazing all around to see if anyone was looking. I tried another pan and hit five more specks of gold.

I had discovered what I had

The hermit's cave, dug into the bank of the Mayo River, about one mile below the hydro dam.

been looking for all my life: the pot of gold at the end of the rainbow. Never again would I work as a wage-slave, fill out time cards or ask my supervisor's permission to go on holidays. I would speak my mind to all the bank managers, landlords, bosses and prickly neighbours I had ever known. I would never ever worry again what anybody thought of me. All because of the hermit's gold.

I quit my job with the power company and went to work on the hermit's claim. My ulcers immediately healed and have never returned. But, although it is hard to believe even yet, not one more speck of gold did I find there. I dug, blasted, sluiced, and tore the back wall from the hermit's cave, to no avail. I think the old geezer dropped that gold where I could find it, and no one has ever been able to discover his lode, although several I know have tried.

I became a gold prospector after that and roamed the valleys and hills of the Yukon for seven years. I turned up gold here and there and but I was really hooked on the search itself. Eventually, I wrote a book about those experiences (Yukon Gold) and have played around at writing and publishing ever since. And though the old hermit is long dead, I really think he gave me the best years of my life.

You can see his bed of gunny sacks, laid upon sand near the window. In the forefront are flat rocks that he appeared to use for crushing ore.

Dry Rice and Road Bumps

I know you folks are tired of the comedy in this column, so this time we're going to be serious and factual.

I just got back from a weekend at Burwash Lodge, where most folks are waiting for the tourists to arrive and the fishing season to start. The fish are so plentiful up that way that you can walk across the rivers on the backs of the fish and not get your feet wet.

Oley, the owner of the Lodge has already hired some help for the season. I saw the huge bags of dried rice in his kitchen. You see, he feeds his help dried rice in the morning and hot water at noon. That way the rice swells up in their bellies and they don't need to eat for the rest of the day.

That's an old Yukon trick that all employers should remember. An easy way to get more work from the help during the long daylight hours is to go around several times a day and set the clocks back a few hours. This is especially effective on newcomers from the south. During the month of June, you could actually get 24 hours work out of them, especially if they nip a few drinks on the job.

The favourite hunting weapon of Kluane folk is a "Forty-Four Tapey," invented by an immigrant from Quebec. It's actually two single-shot .22 calibre rifles taped together with electricians' tape.

Then I heard about the Englishman up there who attends a self-help group so he can stop eating cookies. They've named him the Cookie Monster of Kluane Lake.

The lodge owners along the Kluane route are greatly worried about the highway improvements being built by the Ostashek government. It will have an adverse effect on the economy, they fear.

The way things are, the rough road causes many instances of broken trailer axles and hitches, bent steering systems on RV's, and exhaust systems that come down to engage the surface of the road. Not to mention flat tires and bent rims. When the new road is finished, these repair jobs will cease and all that extra money will go to the USA instead of staying here where it belongs. It's time for all Kluanites to get up a petition against these improvements.

Burwash Lodge is my favourite place to get away from the strife and traffic of Whitehorse. The food is good, rooms are big, comfortable cheap, and the grounds are very historic with lots of old cabins and trails. Be sure to ask about Yukon rates.

But any one of the highway lodges are a great place to sojourn— much more relaxing than a trip Outside and a whole lot cheaper.

Woodcarver Obie of Burlbilly Hill was driving a front-wheel drive Japanese car when he MEEP-MEEPED at a bull moose just south of Burwash Lodge. The bull charged with its antlers down and tore the front grill and fenders right off the car. When the terror-stricken Obie stepped on the gas, the moose took another swipe with its antlers and lopped off the back of the Subaru. Obie arrived at the Lodge unable to speak English or German. It was only through sign language that I got the facts of the story from him.   **S.H.**

Addendum

A couple of weeks ago in this column, I related how a moose tore off the back of this Subaru and how the driver, Obie of Burlbilly Hill, couldn't speak English or German when he got home.

Since then I got a call from him with more details:

It was an **albino** moose that makes tracks that are perfectly square. In fact, Obie follows those tracks when he's looking for firewood because the albino moose knocks down trees wherever it goes, and all Obie has to do is pick up the pieces and take them home for his fire.

TOO MUCH GOLD

Imagine you are in an isolated mountain valley, well away from cities and highways. You have escaped the clutches of human society, with all its clamour for material gain, for security, for conformity. Gone for this day is the accusing stare of a wife who believes you could do much better. Gone is the piercing stare of a boss who might promote you for all your hard work and devotion to his enterprise—or fire you tomorrow.. Gone, just for today, is the feeling that you will never quite fit into it all, no matter how hard you try.

In this lush green valley you walk around for a while, enjoying the solitude. You know you can't stay in this place but just for the hell of it, you push your shovel into the soft gravel, just away from the gurgling stream, and dump it into the pan. The gold pan is full of muck and gravel. You swirl the gravel around in it, around and around, spilling the top layers over the side, till just a little bit of fine sand is left.

Suddenly, something yellow peeps out from the little pile of sand. It is of a colour you have never seen before, but it reminds you of that mysterious brightness of a yellow, harvest moon, seen when you are alone and at a peaceful time in your life. Or, like the yellow hair of the most beautiful, elusive woman in the universe. You reach into the pan and pick that speck up with your fingers, examine it carefully, and then drop into your shirt pocket.

Quickly, you swirl the dirt around in the pan. Another speck of that indefinable yellow jumps clear of the sand then another appears just below it. You pan down to the finest fines until five more specks appear, for a total of seven. After staring at the miracle of it for a while, you stand up and peer all around, to see if anyone is watching, waiting, to steal this treasure away.

No one is in this place but you. You have dropped the shovel and pan and sit by the bank of the little creek, no longer aware of the beautiful surroundings.

"I must get to town and find a map. I must come back, quick, and stake this ground, and then it is mine. The world can go to hell. I'll never have work for a boss again. I'll never have to vacuum or chop salad or listen to how rotten all men (especially whitemen) are. I'll be free!"

All you must do now is wrest this gold from the ground and be yourself again, something you haven't been since early childhood.

And so it is. The ground is yours and the gold comes out of it, bit by bit, from here and there, but never quite enough to keep the world at bay. They want money for food, for equipment, for fuel, and you don't have enough gold to pay for it all.

The answer is simple: look for a better spot, in another valley to the north or south, to the east or west. It has to be there, for gold is everywhere in the Yukon.

And then one day you find lots of gold. The search is over. But you have learned so much by now. You have lived on "rabbit tracks and fish bellies" and became known in the country as a down-and-dirty bum, always on the lookout for another grubstake. But for now, all that is over. You can rejoin the world again. Suddenly, everyone takes you seriously but, you haven't changed, have you? You still have the same thoughts, the same likes and dislikes, so why do they want you now? Because they don't see you as someone with gold, they see you as a moneyed person—a success! Husband material once more!

You let others take over the operation of your claim. They steal your gold while you chase blondes in Vancouver and the game goes on until... one day, you are in a lush green valley, all by yourself, where no one can possibly find you...

Like they say in Alcoholics Anonymous, you can't really know unless you've been there.

The author and Prospector Jim White, hand mining on Glacier Creek, in the rain, in 1984.

Guitars and Bottles

I sill remember the day Hank Williams died. I was five years old at the time and among country folk his tragic passing was such a cataclysmic event and I at such an impressionable age that I have carried Hank's spirit around with me ever since. Through the best of times and through the worst of times, from the Atlantic seaboard to the Yukon, I have listened to his songs and for all these years he has consoled me from the grave, as he has done for many others.

Hank Williams, said to be the greatest folk-singer, song-writer that ever lived, was the product of a domineering, neurotic mother and a weak-willed father who couldn't take it and moved himself into an asylum.

Hank became interested in music when he was a teenager and found himself a wonderful teacher on the streets of his hometown—an old black musician who went by the name of Tee-Tot. Together with Hank's natural lonesomeness and the old black's teachings about rhythm and soul, a talent emerged that would always be totally unique. There was nothing like it before Hank's time; there would nothing like it ever again. A few years later this awesome talent was let loose upon the public.

Musically, he didn't know one note from another and had a voice that was described as being like "the whine of an electric saw going through pine timber." Uneducated, tall and bony, balding at an early age,

he always wore a hat on stage and twisted and swayed as he sang to the crowds. Women went nuts over him. Elvis Presley copied Hank's performing style, added a few twists and became known forever more as Elvis the Pelvis. Hank Williams sang about how he felt, rather than about how he was supposed to feel. That raw honesty would carry him a long way in the entertainment world—and it would speed his way to a very early grave.

In 1949, his recording of "Lovesick Blues" was climbing the charts in the U.S. and Canada. Still, nobody took this unschooled hillbilly very seriously. After a lot of persuading by his promoter, Hank was granted a brief showing at the Grand Ole Opry in Nashville. He already had a reputation as a hard drinker and the Opry managers were reluctant about him from the start.

That night at the Opry the big stars did their numbers and at last Hank Williams' turn came. Hunching his bony frame over the microphone stand and clutching his old guitar, he poured the first verse into the auditorium.

Before that first verse had ended, the audience rose in a great mass from their seats and roared drowning his voice in a standing ovation that brought down the house. Hank smiled, recomposed himself and then really let them have it. At the end of the song the crowd brought him back half a dozen times to sing the last verse. It was the first and only time in Opry history that a performer had been called back so often. To stop the commotion the emcee had to wave the people into a reluctant silence while he made a little speech promising the return of Hank Williams to the show.

Hank's flame was fast reaching its crest. In the next three years MGM released one hit song after another. The air waves danced to Hank William's music, recorded by himself or other singers such as Frankie Lane, Jo Stafford and Polly Bergen. No other song writer had ever had such universal appeal as Hank Williams.

He attained a beautiful wife, a son, a mansion and many Cadillacs, and crowds waited to see him everywhere he performed, whether he was drunk or sober. All too often he kept them waiting, and stumbled onto the stage or didn't appear at all. But the crowds waited anyhow.

As booze took total control of his life, his wife Audrey divorced him and the big music promoters began to shun him. On New Year's Eve, 1953, he died in the back seat of a car, his body so poisoned by alcohol that his heart stopped beating.

Opinion held in those days that addicted drinkers had a moral weakness, that alcoholism was something a person chose for himself, like you would choose a career or a spouse. If Hank were alive today, perhaps, just perhaps, something would be done to help him. But then he might never have written all those sad old songs.

Hank Williams

Sewer Pipe Days

It's kind of nice to be an old geezer and look back on your life. The times I thought were so rough and difficult are now the most fondly remembered. It must like that with a lot of folks.

In my early twenties I fell into a despair over a relationship gone bad. I was walking over the old bridge on Somerset Street in Ottawa when I looked down to see two fellows sitting by the railway track below. They looked up and waved, yelling at me to come on down for a drink. I slid down the steep embankment and joined them beside a big sewer outlet that threw off heat all year round.

One of them was about thirty years old, the other about forty. The older man stood six feet or more and had a raspy, sergeant-major voice. We drank several bottles of wine then laid down in the summer grass for a nap. I woke up ahead of them and went to the nearest wine store and came back with several bottles of Zing (bubbly wine, cost $1 a bottle). It was the start of an adventure that lasted more than two years.

The younger man hanged himself in a rooming house about a week later. That left old Keith and I as partners in despair. We became like a father and son.

He taught me how to jump into a taxi for a trip across town and then dash away without paying but yelling, "Thank you very much, SIR!" We sometimes walked over to Hull, Quebec, where the taverns opened at six in the morning.

Groggy patrons sat around trying to kill their hang-overs from the night before. Keith and I simply went from table to table, downing draft beer until the waiter saw us and we had to leave in a hurry.

Occasionally we found something worth selling and had a few dollars to spend. We then went to the Sally Ann Thrift Shop for nice suits and horn-rimmed glasses. Then it was off to the best hotel that didn't know us.

Keith Milks had the manners of a king. Indeed, he had once commanded an army unit and had been chief electrician for the D.E.W. line. He had owned a huge fleet of taxis in Toronto. We went by cab to view his ex-wife's house in the richest part of the city—it was worth a fortune.

Anyway, we would check into one of the hotels where foreign dignitaries stayed. Somehow, Keith portrayed us as ambassadors waiting for lost luggage and a bank draught and we never had to show any money. Next was room service with steaks and caviar, the very best champagne and female companionship. We sometimes got away with it for three days before we had to slide down the fire escape and go back to skid row.

It was drink, laugh and tell stories (listening, in my case) and wake up sick and hungry. Somehow every day always brought enough food and wine to supply the hoboes with the necessities of life.

Keith panhandled in the morning until we had "entrance fee," which was enough money to sit in a tavern. Then, as often as not, somebody would show up with a bonanza from somewhere. Old Keith would simply take over that person's life until the money was spent.

Behind the parliament buildings in Ottawa are beautiful grounds that overlook the Ottawa River. We had huge wine parties there, with bonfires and storytelling that lasted until everyone passed out and then, as they awoke one by one, they would disappear into the concrete jungle.

I saw ex-circus acrobats who could hand-spring across the grass; I saw magician's tricks that have never been performed elsewhere; I heard some of the finest voices ever to sing an ever-so-sad love song. I saw women with photos of themselves who had been the most beautiful creatures in all the world.

The common theme for every gathering, for every story, for every conversation was this: they spoke only of the past. For them, the present was unbearable and the future was not to be.

Keith disappeared one night into the east side of the city. I asked around and learned that he had been murdered, although the police report said heart failure.

Alcohol took him away from his only son—and then the same poison brought me along as a temporary replacement. That's the only way I can figure why we got along so well. He was a man who had made enemies all his life.

Last winter I made a trip down East and visited some of my old haunts. The Somerset bridge is still the same. The sewer outlet gives off

Above: Somerset railway bridge; below: the cover over the friendly sewer pipe.

its life-saving heat and as I stood there with my camera, I thought I could see Keith Milk's face on the cover. But it probably isn't so. The past is gone from my life and the future beckons warmly. I just wish that some of my old pals had made it with me.

The Humbling Machine

A couple of years ago a friend of mine bought an old printing press. He never found the time to use it so, last summer, I traded him an old Dodge truck for it. All the truck needed was a motor, a transmission, tires and a paint job and it would be as good as new, so I know he got the best of me on that deal.

Some friends helped me wrestle the press into the cabin where I set it up on some steel plates so it wouldn't crash through the floor.

When it comes to machinery, I always thought of myself as being smarter than the average bear. This thing would make my fortune: all I had to do was fire it up and start printing books, magazines, wanted posters, whatever.

Cathy Robertson of *Yukon Instant Printing* (now *Copy/Copy*) was kind enough to come out and give me a half-hour lesson and then I sent for a video tape on running this type of press.

I mentioned what kind of press I had to Sam Cawley of *Willow Printers*. His advice was: "Never turn your back on that model of press."

My first job was to print a book written by a friend of mine. At the Canon dealer I bought some paper at $8 a ream, got some ink and fountain solution and there I was, in the printing business at last.

I filled the input tray with paper, and slopped some black, gooey, sticky ink into the intake holder, threw the switches for the vacuum and air and then fired up the press.

At lightning speed, the pages rushed through to the other side where they heaped up in a tangled mess. Some pages stuck to the blanket roller and worked their way up through all the ink rollers where they disintegrated into a billion shreds of fibre.

In the meantime, the pages rattled through, turning blacker and blacker all the time.

I shut her down and started my first press wash. When I lifted the ink tray off, long goobers of ink left snaky trails all over my lovely press. Pages were tangled in the belts below the press and I had paper everywhere you could see.

Three hours later I looked like the master mechanic in a tar factory but the press was clean.

I started again and the same thing happened.

So I washed it down then fired it up again and the same thing happened, but not right away.

By the tenth try and five thousand pages later, I actually got one page to print.

"I've mastered you now, you son-of-a-b----!"

So I piled a thousand sheets onto the input tray and kept adjusting water, fountain solution, buckle settings, vacuum, air, and so forth. Some pages came out faded, some were too dark and some had little rips in them here and there.

Sometimes I would forget to set just one little lever and all hell would break loose in the little cabin. This old press can make a mess quicker than any five-year-old in his mother's kitchen, believe you me.

It took several trips to the Canon store for paper but I kept at it until one day I printed ten different pages and they all looked pretty fair to me. A real printer wouldn't agree but in the Yukon, these pages were passable.

"I've got you now, you son-of-a-b----!"

My ego returned after the humbling days and weeks of fighting this machine. The weather had turned cold and dry and I learned some lessons about humidity and humility.

In the middle of a run, the old press started whacking and rattling and thumped itself right up off the steel floor plate. By the time I hit the switch, it happened twice more. I figured the whole works was shot.

What happened was that ten or more pages stuck together with static electricity and went through the rollers all together. A vaporizer from Canadian Tire solved that problem and I actually got a book printed (*Ghost Towns & Trails of the Yukon*). If you happen to come across one of those books, you'll know it didn't come easy. Darn that old Sawatsky anyhow.

The beast

The Old Print Shop

Oft-Told Tales

The environmentalists would like to shut down all mining activity in the Yukon. If they succeed, one of the earth's wonderful species will be gone forever—the Yukon prospector. Much of our mythology (aside from our roads and towns) descends from this breed.

A man from Watson Lake, a prospector, had put in a hard winter, as many of his kind have done over the years.

"It was so tough," he said in a woeful voice, "that I woke up one morning to find two dead rats on the floor. And do you know what they died of?"

"No, what?"

"Malnutrition."

This from the old mining town of Mayo, as told by the late Albert Pellon:

The quietest man in the village was old Pierre Gaston. He never gossiped and never got angry. His living came from his old horse and wagon, which he used to haul freight and mail up to the mine at Elsa.

His horse died and he got a new one. When the first riverboat docked at Mayo that spring, old Pierre was there to pick up the mail. Every arrival of a sternwheeler was an important event in Mayo and most of the townfolk came out to see it.

Pierre backed his wagon up to the boat and the crew began heaving mail into it. When the first sack hit the wagon, Pierre's horse reared up and took several steps ahead. He backed it up again and the same thing happened, once, twice, six times or more.

And then came the event that they talk about yet in the mining town of Mayo. Pierre got mad.

"If it wasn't for the women and children here, I'd call you names, you son-of-b----!!!" he said to the horse, in a voice that could be heard for half a mile.

Another tale, told to me by the late mining recorder, Jack Burrows, goes like this:

A miner heard a knock on his cabin door one morning. He opened it to find two young geologists there, wanting to check out his claims—for free; they needed the experience.

"All right," he said, "And when you're finished come back for tea."

Five hours later they knocked again and entered. They had checked his ground and found it to be very poor, they said. In fact, it looked hopeless.

"All right," said the oldtimer, "that's good to know. Now I'll put on the tea."

They noticed the old fellow getting up on a backless chair to put the kettle on the stove.

"Why is that stove up on a platform?" they asked.

"You mean to tell me you don't know?" said the oldtimer. "With all your education and knowledge? And you've said my ground is no good?"

"We still don't know why the stove is up there."

"It's because I didn't have enough stovepipe to reach the ceiling."

My old friend Al Downs decided to live in style at his mining claim on Glacier Creek. He took a mobile home in there and set it up beside the creek. This trailer had a nice kitchen and in the dining room there was a full-length mirror on the wall.

Al left for town and when he got back he noticed the door smashed in and a hole in the outside wall. Further checking revealed that a grizzly bear had broken into the trailer. Old griz' saw himself in that full-length mirror and took off— right through the wall.

You hear so much about thieves these days, especially the kind that break into vehicles. The oldtimers used to take a muskrat trap, file very sharp teeth in it, and chain it to the floor. Then they set the trap under the seat of their truck and left the door unlocked.

Most thieves check under the seat for valuables. In these cases, they would be caught by the muskrat trap and you could hear them holler from anywhere in town. Eventually, the owner of the truck would come back and give this would-be thief a good thrashing while his hand was caught under the seat.

There was an old Frenchman who drove a big Lincoln car down from the silver mine at Elsa to Mayo where he liked to drink in the tavern there. Three times, his car was broken into while he sat in the bar.

So, Frenchy got himself a vicious dog, something like a cross between a wolverine and a pit bull. He always had this dog in the Lincoln with him. When he came down to Mayo to drink, he had the terrible habit of leaving a twenty-dollar bill on the seat of his car, with the window rolled down about six inches. No thief could resist that money. And this old dog of Frenchy's always sat quiet till an arm came through the window. Doctor Clark stitched up more arms than he cared to see and finally put in a complaint about Frenchy's revenge on thieves.

Talking about thieves, Whitehorse was once dotted with little shacks and the denizens of these shacks were rather poor. Mostly because they drank too much. And it was common to steal from your neighbour's woodpile when the weather turned nasty.

Somebody took a little too much of old Ralph L____'s woodpile. He put a sign on it that said, "ONE OF THESE STICKS OF WOOD IS LOADED WITH DYNAMITE."

And he thought that was a smart way to keep the thieves out of his firewood. But, one morning he went out and there was another sign on the woodpile:

"THERE ARE TWO STICKS OF DYNAMITE IN THIS WOODPILE!"

When I last looked, that woodpile was still there, rotting away.

Well, there's some stuff to put in your letters to the folks.

Watch What You Pray For

Did you ever have the feeling you were being watched... you know, like certain women must feel when some guy leers at them on the street? I had that feeling once while I was digging around by the Little Big Salmon River...

I had moved into a little cabin on Lake Creek. It had just enough room for a cot, a stove, a tiny table and one chair. The door was split in two so you could open the top half for fresh air, or, when it was cold, just open the bottom half so the heat wouldn't all leave when you did.

I was running gravel through a sluice box, hoping to get enough gold so I wouldn't have to take a real job. Trouble was, the gravel had clay in it that carried the gold right out the end of the sluice box and at times I felt like shooting myself.

But I kept at it by drying the clay on the creek bank and then running it through with a little more success. Then it started to rain, every day for days and days and I holed up in the cabin trying to make sense of things.

One night as I lay there on the cot, I sent up a prayer to whatever gods there might be in that lonesome valley.

"Wouldn't it be nice if a woman showed up here? I asked. "It wouldn't be quite so lonely, would it?"

Now, anybody that's been over the road will tell you to be careful what you pray for—you might get it.

A couple of nights later I felt the bed moving. Or maybe the whole cabin was shaking a bit. Quickly, I struck a match to the coal-oil lamp and here's what I saw:

A woman was sitting on the end of the bed, with her legs crossed under her, Indian style. I knew she was female just by the look in her eyes.

But she had an awful lot of body hair. In fact, she had a coat of brown greasy hair covering her whole body. It was then I realized: I was looking at a genuine, real-life sasquatch woman!

And from the look in her eyes she was in love with me to boot!

I made a run for the door but she got there ahead of me and blocked it. I gave up on that idea and sat in the chair by the table. She watched me for a while and climbed onto the bed again, still looking at me with those hungry eyes. All I had to do was look toward the door and she leaped across the floor to block it.

As readers of this column know I've been in some tight spots, but this one topped everything. I tried to talk to her, saying, "You don't want me. Anybody in the Yukon will tell you I'll never amount to anything. I don't even have potential. And I'm terrified of intimacy."

But she didn't understand. Just kept staring at me from the bed.

And then I remembered what I

had in my pocket. I took out a roll of money, about two hundred dollars all in small denominations.

I walked over and threw the roll on the bed. She bent over to count the money and I made another run for the door. This time I got there ahead of her. I galloped down the rocky trail to my canoe and leaped aboard, with the paddle flaying water for ten feet as my trembling knees hit the deck.

I never saw that lady again but I heard she teamed up with some guy in Carmacks who likes hairy women. (I think Windy Farr of Dawson City had a similar experience and if he were alive he could confirm the facts of this case but...)

On Being Yourself

When I first arrived in the Yukon, I found myself fascinated with the characters I met here. They seemed to have a serenity about them, a wisdom, that southerners couldn't attain. It was some years later that I discovered their secret.

In the Yukon, *they could be themselves.* And really, no person can be truly happy until they learn to do that. But also, you have to live where being yourself is allowed.

The City of Whitehorse has become a copy of any small city you might find in the south. Most of the great characters that once prowled the streets are gone, either to Jim Robb's Colourful Five Percent heaven—or they have moved on.

Part of the reason is that Whitehorse has the tightest set of bylaws you might find in any city in the world. They have laws governing everything from the woodpile in front of your shack to that old "parts truck" in your backyard. In short, you can't really live there in any sort of comfort.

So, people like Brittlebones, Stampede John, Tom the Banker, Buzz-saw Jimmy, Wigwam Harry, Steamboat Mary, Two-Man McDonald, and the other great citizens of the past will likely never walk the streets of Whitehorse again.

Anyway, the years have passed too quickly and I found myself wishing I could find some of the oldtime Yukon characters, but where did they go?

This past summer, I started patronizing the **Carcross Corner Cafe.** The food and coffee are very good, very reasonably priced, and a lot of my friends eat there.

We traded stories about the good old days, but also some newer gossip. Like the couple who shared one set of false teeth, who went to a wedding feast where the wife was heard shouting at her husband to *"hand over those teeth; you've had them long enough!"*

I heard hunting stories, prospecting stories, stories about some of the characters we all knew. In fact, we were talking about our contemporaries.

And then one day, I looked around the cafe. The fellows here were all about my age! They seemed to have that look about them that I admired so much in the Yukon oldtimers.

We are the characters now. Someday the young folk will come to us for advice and stories. And the first thing we'll tell them is to "keep the expenses down and don't worry about what anybody thinks."

To paraphrase Thoreau:

"Let each person march to the drum that they hear, however measured or far away."

Carcross Corner Cafe

A Foggy Moose Hunt

Last fall I had a strange experience while moose-hunting by boat down the Teslin River. I had camped on the riverbank for the night and found fresh moose tracks leading up a mountain on the east side of the river.

I followed those tracks, up and up and up till I got past the tree-line and saw a huge moose out in the open. Bang, bang, down it went and then I realized my mistake: how was I going to get the meat down to my boat?

It turned dark up there on the mountain and I could feel big snowflakes hitting my face like cold kisses. Then a thick fog rolled up the sidehill from the river below.

So there I was in the dark, fogged in and vibrating from the cold. Rather than freeze to death waiting for daylight, here's what I did: I sliced the belly open and rolled the guts out of that old moose; then I crawled inside for the night. Nice and warm. Moist, too.

I was dreaming about my mother when I felt something tugging at the moose. I opened the belly flap just a bit and peeked outside. A pack of a dozen or more wolves surrounded me, looking like they were about to eat the moose and me with it. But then I realized: we were moving! Those wolves had that moose on the drag!

From inside the moose's belly, I caught hold of the tailbone with one hand and the Adam's apple with the other and found out I could steer that thing. You know, like using the rudder on your boat.

With the wolves dragging it at a full gallop, I steered that moose right down to my boat. Then I jumped out and shot one of the wolves and the rest scattered in all directions.

I floated downriver till I got to Carmacks where I had left my truck. In the Carmacks Hotel I sold the wolf-hide to a German tourist. Then I tossed the meat into my old Dodge and drove home.

Windy Farr of Dawson had a similar experience some years ago so I guess it can happen to anybody. If you find yourself steering a moose, don't forget how to grab the tailbone and neckbone from the inside, and you'll be home with the meat in no time at all.